CLAIMING MY UNTOUCHED MISTRESS

HEIDI RICE

MILLS & BOON

First Published in Great Britain 2019
by Mills & Boon, an imprint of HarperCollins*Publishers*
1 London Bridge Street, London, SE1 9GF

ISBN: 978-0-263-27050-1

FSC
www.fsc.org
MIX
Paper from
responsible sources
FSC C007454

This book is produced from independently certified FSC™ paper
to ensure responsible forest management.
For more information visit www.harpercollins.co.uk/green.

Printed and bound in Spain
by CPI, Barcelona

To my gorgeous husband, Rob,
whose love of Texas Hold 'Em
finally became useful in my writing career!

CHAPTER ONE

I STRUGGLED TO control the tidal wave of panic surging through me as I read the sign on Dante Allegri's Monaco casino.

Welcome to The Inferno

The glitter of lights gave the building's imposing eighteenth-century façade a fairy-tale glow in the Mediterranean night—making me feel like even more of a fraud in the second-hand designer gown and uncomfortable ice-pick heels my sister and I had sourced online. What I was about to do could make or break my family.

Please God, don't let Dante Allegri be in the house tonight.

I'd seen photos of Allegri, and read myriad articles about him in the last month as I prepared for this night. He scared me as a competitor but terrified me as a woman.

Allegri was famous for his ruthlessness, having risen from the slums of Naples to create a billion-dollar empire of casinos in Europe and the US. If I had to play against him, and he figured out the system I had developed, he would show me no mercy.

A sea breeze from the marina below the casino lifted the tendrils of hair off my neck which had escaped the elaborate up-do my sister had spent hours constructing from my unruly curls. Shivers racked my body, but I knew it wasn't the warm summer night that was making me feel so cold inside—it was fear.

Stop standing here like a dummy and move.

Lifting the hem of the gown, I walked up the marble stairs to the main entrance, making an effort to keep my back straight and my gaze forward. The million-dollar bank draft borrowed from my brother-in-law's loan shark stashed in the jewelled clutch purse on my wrist felt as if it weighed several tons.

'You want to throw good money after bad, that's your choice, Ms Trouvé, but I'll be here tomorrow to collect, whatever happens.'

The words of Brutus Severin, Carsoni's muscle man, echoed in my head and the chill spread like a frost.

This was my last chance to free us from the threats and intimidation, the possibility of losing not just our family home, but also our dignity and self-respect. Something my sister Jude's husband Jason had stolen from us twelve months ago—after losing a fortune at Allegri's roulette tables.

Failure simply was not an option tonight.

I approached the security detail standing guard at the entrance and passed them my ID card. I prayed that Carsoni's forger had done the job we had paid him for. The guard nodded and passed it back to me. But my panic refused to subside.

What if my system didn't work? Or had more tells than I had anticipated. I wasn't sure if I'd had enough time to test it properly—and I had never had the opportunity to test it against players of Allegri's calibre. How did I know it would stand up to scrutiny? I was a maths prodigy, not a poker player, for goodness' sake.

The buy-in for tonight's game was a staggering one million euros. And it was one million euros I could not afford to lose.

If Allegri was here, and decided to play—as he occasionally did, according to my research—and he beat me, not only would Belle Rivière be lost for ever, but I would owe Carsoni an extra million euros I couldn't repay. Because the sale of the property, now we'd already mortgaged it and sold all our other valuables and most of the furniture, would only cover the balance of Jason's losses and the astronomical interest Carsoni had been charging us since the night Jason had disappeared.

Please, I'm begging you, God. Don't let Allegri be here.

The door guard signalled to a tall, good-looking man standing at the entrance to the main floor. He joined us.

'Welcome to The Inferno, Miss Spencer,' the man said. 'I'm Joseph Donnelly, the casino manager. We have you listed as one of tonight's club buy-ins.' He sent me a quizzical look, obviously not used to having someone of my age and gender join the casino's exclusive weekly poker tournament. 'Is that correct?'

I nodded, trying to channel my inner elite, entitled heiress—something I had never been, even though my mother had been the granddaughter of a French count.

'I've heard The Inferno's game is one of the most challenging,' I said. 'I was hoping Allegri would be here tonight,' I lied smoothly—playing the pampered rich girl to the hilt. If life with my mother had taught me one thing, before she died, it was how to appear confident when I felt the opposite.

'Appearances are everything, ma petite chou. *If they think you are one of them, you cannot fail.'*

The casino manager sent me an easy smile, and I waited for the words I hoped to hear—that my research had paid off and Dante was in Nice this evening, wining and dining the model he had been linked with for several weeks in the celebrity press.

'Dante's here tonight; I'm sure he'd relish the challenge.' Donnelly's words didn't register at first, and then they slammed into me.

No. No. No.

I pasted a smile on my face, the same smile I had worn at my mother's funeral to receive the condolences of journalists who had hounded her throughout her life, while coping with the body blow of fresh grief.

My movements were stiff though, as Donnelly led me to the teller's booth to deposit the stake I had borrowed at two thousand per cent interest. The stake I couldn't afford to lose.

I ran all the possibilities over in my mind. Could I back out now? Make up some fictitious excuse? Pretend I was sick? Because that wasn't a lie—my stomach was churning like a storm at sea.

Allegri was one of the best poker players in the world. Not only could I lose all the money but if he figured out my system he could have me banned from every reputable casino. So I'd have no chance of ever recovering Jason's losses.

Even as my frantic mind tried to grasp and dissect all the possibilities though, I knew I couldn't back out. I'd taken a chance Allegri wouldn't be here and I'd lost. But I had to go through with tonight's game.

Before I had a chance to handle the visceral fear at the thought of facing Allegri with so much at stake, a deep voice reverberated down my spine.

'Joe, Matteo tells me all the players have arrived.'

I swung round and came face to face with the man who had haunted my dreams—and most of my waking hours—

for months, ever since I'd begun working on this scheme to free our family from debt. To my shock, Allegri was even taller, broader and more devastatingly handsome in the flesh than he had been in the numerous celebrity blogs and magazines I'd been monitoring.

I knew he was only thirty, but the harsh angles of his face, and the unyielding strength of muscle and sinew barely contained by the expensive tuxedo, made it clear that the softness and inexperience of youth—if he had ever been young or soft—had left him long ago. Everything about him exuded power and confidence, and a frightening arrogance. No, not arrogance. Arrogance implied a sense of entitlement beyond one's abilities. This man was fully aware of his abilities, and was ready to use them with complete ruthlessness.

His vivid blue gaze flickered over my face—and one dark eyebrow raised a fraction of a centimetre. The tiny tell vanished as soon as it had appeared. His intense gaze took a quick tour down my body. The provocative dress became instantly transparent while at the same time squeezing the air out of my lungs, as if the thin satin had turned to cast iron and was tightening around my ribs like a piece of medieval torture equipment.

Unlike the looks I had experienced from Carsoni and his men over the last year though, Dante Allegri's perusal didn't cause revulsion but something much more disturbing. A heavy weight sunk low into my abdomen and sensation prickled over my skin as if I were being stroked by an electric current. His attention was exhilarating and enervating, pleasurable and painful all at the same time. My reaction shocked me, because I couldn't seem to control it. My thighs trembled, my breasts swelled against the bodice of my medieval torture equipment and it took an effort of titanic proportions to stop my breathing from speeding up.

'That's correct, Dante,' Joseph Donnelly replied to his boss. 'This is Edie Spencer,' he added, wrenching me out of the trance Allegri's presence had caused. 'She's just arrived and is hoping to play you tonight.'

I winced at the amusement in Donnelly's tone, my panic increasing to go with the inexplicable aches all over my body. As if it wasn't bad enough that I had tossed myself into the lion's den tonight, I had decided to poke the lion with that foolish boast.

Allegri didn't look particularly impressed as his intense gaze roamed over my face.

'Exactly how old are you, Miss Spencer?' he asked, addressing me directly for the first time. His English was perfect, the accent a mid-Atlantic hybrid of American and British with barely a hint of his native Italian. 'Are you even legally allowed to be here?' he added, and I bristled at the condescension. It was a long time since I'd felt like a child, let alone been treated like one.

'Of course—I'm twenty-one,' I said in a show of defiance that probably wasn't wise, but something about the way he was looking at me—as if he actually saw me—and the disturbing conflagration of sensation that look was setting off all over my body made me bold.

He continued to stare at me, as if he were trying to see into my soul, and I forced myself not to break eye contact.

The noise from the main floor of the casino, as Europe's billionaire elite tried their luck at roulette and *vingt-et-un*, faded to a distant hum under his intense scrutiny—until all I could hear was the thunder of my own heartbeat thumping my ribs.

'How long have you been playing Texas Hold 'Em, Miss Spencer?' he asked at last, mentioning the variety of poker all professional players favoured.

With five 'community' cards turned face up in the mid-

dle of the table, and two 'hole' cards dealt face down to each player, Texas Hold 'Em required the greatest amount of skill in calculating probabilities and assessing risk as you formed your hand from your two 'hole' cards and the five 'community' cards, and the least amount of dumb luck. And that's where my system came in. I had developed a mathematical formula to assess the betting behaviour of the other players, which would give me an advantage as the game went on. But if I was spotted using the formula I would be in trouble, just like players who were caught counting cards when playing Black Jack.

Once the casinos figured out how to spot those players they were banned for life, their winnings forfeit—even though what they were doing wasn't strictly speaking cheating. I couldn't risk either of those scenarios.

'Long enough,' I answered, forcing myself to pretend a confidence I didn't feel.

My mother had been right about one thing. Appearances were everything now. If I wanted to win, I couldn't show this man a single weakness. Appearing confident and in control was as important as *being* confident and in control. In fact, letting him believe I was over-confident would also work to my advantage—the ultimate double bluff, because then he would underestimate me.

His devastating face remained impassive, but the glitter of heat in his irises and the tiny tensing of his jaw, which drew my eyes to a scar on his upper lip, suggested that my cocky statement had hit its mark. I would have felt more triumphant about his reaction if that quickly masked tell hadn't increased the weight in the pit of my abdomen by several hundred pounds—and the prickle of awareness coasting over my skin by several thousand volts.

What was happening to me? I had never had a response like this to any man.

'I guess we'll see about that, Miss Spencer,' he said, then turned to his casino manager. 'Escort Miss Spencer up to the Salon, Joe. Introduce her to tonight's other Millionaire Club players.' He glanced at his watch, all business again, even though the vibes coming off him—of heat and animosity—were turning my legs to jelly.

'I need to speak to Renfrew but I'll be up in thirty minutes,' he added. 'We can kick off then.'

'You're joining the table tonight?' Donnelly asked, sounding mildly surprised.

'Yes,' he said, that deep voice stroking the hot spot which had started to throb at my core. 'I never back down from a challenge, especially one issued by a beautiful woman.'

It took me a moment to realise *I* was the beautiful woman, probably because the glare he sent me before he walked away suggested he didn't consider it a compliment.

But as I was led away by the casino manager towards a bank of elevators, I couldn't take my eyes off Allegri's retreating back. His broad shoulders looked indomitable, and yet terrifyingly alluring in the expertly tailored designer evening suit. The crowd parted to allow his dark figure to stride through the room.

I had to win tonight, no matter what the cost—my family's future depended on it. But as the inexplicable heat continued to throb at my core, my senses thrown into turmoil by that one brief encounter, I had the agonising suspicion I had already lost.

CHAPTER TWO

EDIE SPENCER WAS an enigma I couldn't solve, and it was driving me nuts.

We'd been playing for over three hours now and I couldn't figure out her system. I was even finding it hard to read her tells—those insignificant physical responses every player had which they were unaware of, but which made them an open book when it came to assessing their next move. And the reason why I couldn't figure out her tells was as simple as it was surprising. I couldn't concentrate on the game—because I was too busy concentrating on her.

While her winnings had been modest so far, they had been building steadily, unlike every other player at the table, who had the inevitable troughs that came with a game of chance. I'd managed to dispose of all but one of the other players, so there were only three of us left at the table. But while my friend Alexi Galanti, the Formula One owner who sat beside her, was down to his last million, Edie Spencer was sitting with a tidy pile of chips in front of her that matched my own.

I knew she had to be using a system which was even more ingenious than mine. But my desire to figure it out was a great deal less urgent than my desire to peel her out of the provocative dress she wore. The lace that covered her cleavage was doing nothing to distract me from the tempting display of soft female flesh beneath.

'Raise, two hundred,' Alexi said as he tossed a couple of hundred thousand euro chips on the table, raising the stake after the blind bids.

I stifled my frustration as I watched Edie's slim fingers lift her hole cards on the table to study them again.

I wanted Alexi out of the game so I could play Miss Spencer alone. But Alexi was a good player. So I needed to concentrate on the play, and not the provocative display of cleavage across the table.

I stifled the visceral tug of anticipation, and the swift tug of arousal, at the prospect of having her all to myself. Mixing sex with poker was never a good strategy. But as I watched her I had to admit it wasn't just her beauty that had been driving me nuts for hours.

I'd seen a spark of fire downstairs, when I'd questioned her about her age, and it had excited me. For the first time in a long time, I'd found myself relishing the challenge of playing a stimulating game with a stimulating woman. But ever since that moment downstairs, I hadn't been able to tempt that spark out of hiding again.

Her skin had remained pale and unflushed, her hands folded demurely in her lap when she wasn't betting or checking her cards, her breathing even. Her bright green gaze, which had captivated me downstairs, hadn't connected with mine since.

And while that lack of eye contact was frustrating enough when it came to reading her play, what was a great deal more frustrating was that I was becoming even more turned on. Not less so. And even more desperate to see that flash of green fire again.

I didn't like it. I never let physical desire distract me at the table, but what I liked even less was the fact I didn't understand what it was about her I found so hot.

For starters, she was only twenty-one years old. And she looked even younger. When I had first seen her, I would have placed her as nineteen, twenty at the most, the revealing dress and heavy eye make-up making her wide emerald eyes and slim coltish figure look for a moment like a child playing dress up.

Young women were not to my taste. I preferred women older than me as a rule, women with lots of experience, who could match my appetites in bed, provide stimulating conversation out of it—and didn't get over-invested in the relationship, or over-emotional when I gave them an expensive bauble to send them on their way.

I had also never had the desire before to pursue a woman who was not sending me clear signals she was interested in a little bed sport too. The truth was, when younger women bought into the high stakes game they were usually looking for a little of both—the chance to test their skill at the table and test their skills in my bed. A temptation I had found it very easy to resist up till now.

But not this time.

Of course it was more than possible Miss Spencer's demure behaviour was all an act, intended to intrigue and entice me. If that were the case, I had to give her credit for trying a new tactic. But that still didn't answer the question of why it was working so effectively.

Was it simply the enigma of her? Or that momentary spark of defiance? Or maybe it was the challenge she represented? How long had it been since I had found a woman this hard to read?

As I studied her debating her play, unable to detach my gaze from her, I forced myself to focus.

This girl was no different from the many other heiresses

I had met over the years while I was setting up my business. The spoilt, entitled daughters of millionaire businessmen and aristocrats, European royalty and Arab sheikhs, who had never had to work a day in their lives and didn't know the meaning of want. They played the tables to imbue their lives with the excitement their pointless existences lacked—without realising that if money had no value, the risk and the pay-off of gambling with it would have no value too.

But despite my determination to dismiss and rationalise her unprecedented effect on me, my gaze continued to roam over her, the embers of my fascination burning in my abdomen.

Her skin glowed with youth in the subtle lighting, the plunging V of her gown beneath the lace highlighting full firm breasts flushed with an alabaster softness. The ruched peaks of her nipples, outlined through the satin, were the only response she seemed unable to control.

I would have taken some satisfaction from that… But the increasingly relentless desire to ease the edge of her gown down, expose those peaks and feel them swell and elongate against my tongue wasn't making me feel particularly impressed with my own control.

'Fold,' she said, passing her hole cards to Alexi, who was dealing—and eluding my attempts to force her to break cover, again.

I bit down on my tongue to stop the curse coming out of my mouth, like a damn rookie. But, as if she had sensed my frustration, her gaze flicked to mine.

It flicked away again almost immediately. But in that moment, as our gazes locked, I saw that flash of fire. A jolt of heat eddied through my system.

Her chest rose and fell and then stilled as she regained her composure. But the pebbled outline of her nipples became more prominent against the satin.

Desire flared in my abdomen like a meteor shower, as I finally solved at least some of the puzzle. The veneer of composure was just that—a veneer.

Whatever system Edie had devised, she had just exposed one major weakness.

Maybe she was still an enigma in some ways. But one thing I knew now with complete certainty—she was as hungry for me as I was for her. And for some reason she wanted to hide it. Which gave me the upper hand, because it was a weakness I could exploit.

Hot blood surged in my groin.

In fact, it was a weakness I was going to take great pleasure in exploiting.

Game on, bella.

CHAPTER THREE

He knows.

I had made a terrible mistake. I knew it as soon as my gaze met Allegri's and held for a nanosecond too long.

I'd been avoiding eye contact all night, that penetrating blue gaze turning my stomach to molten lava and making my nipples tighten every time it caught mine.

I didn't understand my reaction to him. The only thing I did know was that I couldn't let him see it—or I would be completely at the mercy of it, and him. But the more I tried to control my physical responses, the harder they became to hide. And the more difficult I found it to keep my mind on the game.

I should have bet on that hand. I knew the probability he had a better one was fractionally greater than mine, given the way he had betted during the blinds, but if I never tested him, never lost, he would begin to suspect I had a system. The problem was, I had been avoiding going head to head with him all night, the fear of exposing the strange currents gripping my body too great to risk it.

But as soon as I'd folded again, and saw his jaw tense, the rush of exhilaration at frustrating him was like a drug, intoxicating me. As a result I had been incapable of stopping myself from lifting my head and staring directly at him.

He remained calm, the tensing of his jaw easing, and

then his lips curved in a sensual smile that fed the rush of adrenaline.

I ripped my gaze away before he could see more. But I knew it was already too late. The giddy longing must have been written all over my face.

My breathing stopped. It just stopped. I had to fight for the next breath, but as I forced my lungs to function in an even rhythm again, my nipples became so hard they felt as if they were going to poke right through my dress.

I listened to the play continue around me, as Allegri finished off Galanti. The motor-racing entrepreneur subsided with good grace, throwing his pair of aces down with a hollow laugh when Allegri turned over his winning hand—a two to match the pair of twos already on the table.

'Damn it, Dante, one of these days, I swear your luck will run out,' Galanti said.

'Keep dreaming, Alexi,' Allegri said as he began methodically stacking the pile of chips he'd won.

Galanti cast a look my way as he knocked back the last of his whisky. 'Maybe Miss Spencer has your number?' Standing to leave the table, he offered me his hand. 'You've been an impressive and beautiful opponent, Edie,' he said with deliberate familiarity, the look in his eyes flirtatious.

'Thank you, Mr Galanti,' I said. As we shook hands, I tried to figure out why I had no reaction to this man and yet was finding it so hard to control the one I had to Allegri.

'Good luck,' Galanti said. 'Maybe we could meet afterwards for a drink?' he added. 'I'm going to try my luck at the roulette table next, so I'll be around to celebrate with you when you beat this bastard.'

The vote of confidence surprised me, but the invitation surprised me more—I made an effort to make myself invisible whenever I was around men. Both Jude and

I had learned instinctively to shy away from male attention, thanks to the endless stream of lovers my mother had brought into our lives as teenagers.

The decision to decline Galanti's invitation was instant and unequivocal. But as I opened my mouth to cry off, Allegri spoke.

'Get lost, Alexi. Miss Spencer is out of bounds—she's all mine now.'

Galanti laughed and left, apparently unaware of the subtle edge in Allegri's voice. But I'd heard it, along with the hint of possessiveness.

She's all mine now.

What was that supposed to mean?

I made the mistake of looking at him again, and my blood pressure spiked on cue. He was watching me, the way he had been all night. But, instead of frustration, all I saw now was satisfaction, and challenge, daring me to react to his outrageous remark.

He finished shuffling the cards, his strong wrists and capable fingers flexing in practised motion, never taking his gaze off me.

The tension in the room increased as the door closed behind Galanti, leaving us alone in the plush salon. The huge mullioned window gave us a spectacular view of the bay, the boats moored in the marina adding a sprinkle of lights to the dark sea, but the overwhelmingly masculine space, luxuriously furnished in leather and mahogany in accents of green and brown, suddenly seemed dangerous… And exciting.

Allegri had dismissed the serving staff over an hour ago. At the time it had seemed a generous gesture—it had been past midnight. But now we were alone together I was wondering if he had planned it.

For the first time, the strange melting sensation at my

core and the panic it caused was joined by a spark of anger at his proprietary comment to Galanti.

I'd spent the last year of my life being bullied and belittled by Carsoni and his hired muscle—I didn't like it.

'I'd prefer it if you didn't make decisions for me, Mr Allegri,' I said, in as placid a voice as I could muster while I was burning up with indignation.

'And what decision would that be?' he asked, cutting the pack one-handed.

'The decision to have a drink with Mr Galanti,' I huffed, indignation getting the better of me.

'As you had already decided to give him the brush-off,' he said, 'I hardly think I took the decision away from you.'

He cut the cards again, and smiled that sensual smile—which did diabolical things to my heart rate. The arrogant comment rattled me, but it infuriated me more, loosening my tongue.

'Actually, I hadn't decided to give him the brush-off,' I lied.

'Yes, you had,' he said with complete confidence. The slight curve of his lip unsettled and confused me—was he amused by my futile attempt to misdirect him?

And how the heck did he know I had been planning to give Galanti the brush-off?

'How could you possibly know that?' I blurted out.

His blue gaze darkened and, to my horror, an answering heat hit my chest and spread across my collarbone like a rash.

'Because he's not your type, *bella*,' he said. The gruff tone, and his easy use of the endearment, made the rash spread up my neck and hit my cheeks. 'I am.'

CHAPTER FOUR

THE DESIRE I had been trying and failing to control for hours shot through my system like a fine wine, but I was through caring about it as Edie Spencer's gaze finally flashed the green fire I had witnessed downstairs.

Welcome back, bella.

Satisfaction joined with the intoxicating jolt of power and passion as I saw indignation flush her pale skin. The challenging light heated her eyes to a sparkling emerald. She really was exquisite. Provocative, fearless and, from the system I had yet to fully fathom, also wildly intelligent. Whatever game she was playing, she was proving to be a worthy opponent. Not something I was used to when it came to the spoilt children of the rich.

I was going to have a great deal of fun winning this game—and then mining the sexual chemistry we so clearly shared. If she was anywhere near as hot in bed as she was at the table, this was liable to be a very entertaining night.

'You're extremely arrogant, Mr Allegri,' she said, but I caught the catch of breath in her throat as she said it. 'Perhaps you should concentrate on the game, instead of my fictitious attraction to your charms.'

'I happen to be very good at multi-tasking,' I replied as I placed the pack on the table, suddenly less interested in dealing the cards than I was in dealing with her. 'I can play and read your responses at the same time—which is how I know it's me you want, not Alexi.'

'What responses?' she said, her chest rising and falling again in an erratic rhythm. 'I don't have any response to you, whatever your ego might be telling you.'

I decided not to argue the point. I simply let my gaze drift down to her nipples and watched them swell against the satin. I could only imagine how desperate she must be now for relief. The peaks begging for the sharp strong tug of my lips. Some women were extremely sensitive there; I would hazard a guess she was one of them from the way the flush she'd kept at bay for three hours spread across her collarbone under my examination.

'How about we test that theory,' I said, 'and take a recreational break?'

She stiffened, but the blush was out of control now. And all the more arresting for it.

She didn't respond so I added, 'We've been playing for three hours—and I'm starving.' I let the implication hang in the air that it wasn't just food I was hungry for—while enjoying her attempts to stifle the now livid blush rioting across those pale cheeks.

I saw her debate my request, unsure whether to take the bait or not. If she knew anything about me at all—and I would hazard a guess she had done more than her fair share of research on my habits from her play so far—she would know I frequently played for twenty-four hours straight without the need for sustenance. I didn't get hungry during a match, all my focus on the turn of the cards. But right now I was distracted, so why not run with it? After all, that delectable flash of temper and heat in her eyes was even more challenging than her play.

I wondered exactly how bold she really was.

Would she play it safe and decline my offer? Keep her

cards close to her chest and continue to deny the chemistry making both our bloods boil? Or would she take the risk of exposing her own hunger, to get the upper hand in the game of cat and mouse we were now playing?

I was hoping it would be the latter, but had I overestimated her daring?

I thought I probably had when she looked away and I saw her throat move as she swallowed.

But then, to my surprise, she turned back to me and those mesmerising emerald eyes sparked with defiance—and a steely determination.

'I'd love a supper break,' she said, the tiny quiver in her voice contradicted by the thrust of her nipples and the flagrant colour still flaring on her cheeks. 'But only because I'm hungry and I need all my energy to concentrate on beating you.'

'Touché, bella.' I chuckled, enjoying her audacious threat, and the sparkle of green fire. I picked up my cellphone and texted Joe to get a meal up here pronto. She hadn't just taken the bait; she'd swallowed it whole then spat it back out again.

Why that should make me relish bedding her even more than beating her was probably a little perverse—as a rule I never slept with an opponent, however tempted—mixing poker with sexual pleasure could get complicated fast… But, right now, my goal was a simple one. Stoke the hunger between us until she gave up all her secrets.

Then I could make quick work of defeating her at the table—and we could both reap the rewards.

CHAPTER FIVE

HAD I COMPLETELY lost my ever-loving mind?

Why had I agreed to stop play and share a meal with Dante Allegri? It was stupid and reckless to the point of being extremely dangerous—especially if you factored in the pheromones rioting through my body every time he so much as glanced at me.

But I didn't realise how dangerous my situation was until I was sitting opposite him at a table in the adjoining salon, set with sparkling crystal, fine china and antique silverware. His devilishly handsome face—illuminated by the flicker of candlelight—looked more savage than suave as the prickles of sensation all over my skin refused to subside.

It was as if my body had a death wish.

He lifted my plate to serve me from the banquet displayed on a sideboard which had been brought up from the casino kitchens by a troop of waiters who, to my dismay, had disappeared again almost immediately.

'What's your pleasure, Miss Spencer?' The formal address sounded ridiculous, given the way I could feel his voice caressing my skin as he spoke my name in that husky, amused tone.

Wake up, Edie. This isn't real...he's not interested in you... He's a practised seducer trying to use his industrial-strength sex appeal to weaken all your defences.

I shouted the mantra in my head as I fought the strange sensation—a mesmerising mix of lethargy and fizzing urgency—which had taken over my body and drawn me into this perilous position.

I should have resisted the urge to challenge him, to provoke him and to accept the gauntlet he'd thrown down, but I was here now and I couldn't back down so I'd just have to play out this hand to the best of my abilities. Maybe I'd had some vague notion of playing him at his own game but, as the intimacy drew in around me and my ribs contracted around my thundering heartbeat, I realised the recklessness of that knee-jerk decision. I had no experience at all of men, especially not rich, powerful, sexually magnetic men who exuded the kind of confidence and charisma Dante Allegri did without even trying. I might as well have been a mouse, trying to impress a lion.

I breathed in the delicious aroma of the food as I concentrated on choosing a selection but, as my mouth watered and my stomach grumbled, I'd never felt less like eating.

I picked a few dishes from the lavish array of French cuisine—which I noted was plentiful enough to have fed me and my sister for a week—only to find myself entranced by the play of his strong capable hands as he ladled the fragrant samples of delicately spiced fish and lightly steamed vegetables, the rich gratin and colourful salads onto a gold-rimmed fine china plate.

He had wide callused palms and long fingers and blunt, carefully clipped nails. His skin looked darkly tanned against the pristine white cotton of his shirt. He'd lost the tuxedo jacket several hours ago but before serving me he had rolled up his shirt sleeves, giving me a disturbing view of the corded muscles in his forearms, the sprinkle of dark hair, as he placed my plate on the table.

He proceeded to serve himself a large helping, then sat

down opposite me. He lifted a bottle of wine out of the ice bucket set next to the table and uncorked it in a few efficient strokes, then tipped the bottle towards my glass.

'Some wine? I assure you this white goes well with Argento's skate *au beurre noir.*'

Drinking probably wasn't a good idea, but with my heart battering my chest at approximately five hundred beats per second I had to do something to slow it down, so I nodded.

He poured me a shallow glass, not enough to get me drunk, I realised with relief, but as he served himself I noticed the bottle's label. A Mouton Rothschild Blanc from the turn of the new century. I took a generous gulp to hide my surprise, letting the fresh, delightfully fruity taste moisten my dry mouth.

I wondered why he hadn't boasted about the wine, which I knew sold for thousands of euros a bottle, because one of the many things we had been forced to do after my mother died, to pay off her debts, was auction everything in her wine cellar.

'Buon appetito,' he said, nodding to my plate before picking up his own cutlery.

I scooped up a mouthful of buttery fish and creamy potatoes, but I could barely taste it as I swallowed. He was still watching me. Assessing my weaknesses, I was sure, with that focused, intensely blue gaze as he devoured his own food.

'Where are you from, Miss Spencer?' he asked finally. He leaned back in his chair and lifted his wine glass to those sensual lips.

I watched him swallow and took another sip from my own glass as I gave up trying to eat the food and attempted to come up with a convincing answer.

Unfortunately I hadn't prepared for this eventuality,

having convinced myself Allegri wouldn't even be in the house tonight.

'A small town north of Chantilly. Lamorlaye,' I said, mentioning a town close enough to Belle Rivière that I would know the details, just in case he knew the area too.

'You're French?' His eyes narrowed as his brows rose up his forehead. 'And yet you speak English without an accent.'

'I'm half-French, half-British,' I clarified, my heartbeat stuttering under that inquisitive gaze. I knew it was always best to keep as close to the truth as possible, because then it was harder to get caught out in a lie, but I didn't want to give him information that might make it possible to track me down after I won tonight's game… *If* I won tonight's game.

The jolt of panic had me taking another sip of my wine to calm the nerves that were jiggling around in my stomach with Argento's skate.

'I live most of the year in Knightsbridge,' I said, plucking the most expensive area of London I could think of out of thin air. 'But the city is so stifling at this time of year,' I continued, lying through my teeth now to put him off the scent. I needed to sound urbane and cosmopolitan and a little bored to keep up the pretence that I was a rich heiress amusing herself for the summer. 'So I prefer to stay at my parents' estate in Lamorlaye from May to September… The social scene in Chantilly is so much more exclusive and refined than Paris, and our chateau has a pool and a tennis court and a cinema so I can keep in shape and entertain myself when I'm not socialising or making flying visits to Monaco, or Cannes, or Biarritz.'

'You don't work?' He sounded both suspicious and unimpressed.

I slipped my hands off the table and rested them in my lap, rubbing the calluses on my palms I'd been hiding all evening. The last thing I wanted him to know about was the night-time cleaning jobs I'd taken on in the last year—along with the accountancy work I'd been doing for local businesses ever since my mother died four years ago. If he knew how desperate I was to win this game, it would only make me easier prey.

'Work's so overrated, don't you think?' I said. 'And anyway, I'd hate to be tied down like that. I'm a free spirit, Mr Allegri. I much prefer the danger of riding my luck at the roulette table or the excitement of calculating my odds during a game of Texas Hold 'Em than shackling myself to a boring nine-to-five job,' I continued, the lies floating out of my mouth like confetti at a high society wedding—the sort I'd only ever seen in magazines or on the Internet.

His frown lowered and for a split second I thought I'd overdone the rich airhead act. He had to know I wasn't an idiot from the way I'd played so far. But then the crease in his brow eased and a cynical, knowing smile curved those wide sensual lips. But while my panic at being caught in a lie downgraded, what I saw flicker across his face for a split second had my heart bouncing back into my throat.

Disappointment.

When he spoke again, his voice rich with condescension, I was convinced I must have imagined it. Surely, like all the rich men I'd ever met, he preferred his women pretty and vacuous—the way my mother had always taken great pains to appear when trying to attract a new 'protector'.

'From the way you play poker,' he said, faint praise evident in every syllable, 'I'd say your time has been very well spent.'

Picking up my glass, I toasted him with unsteady hands. *'Touché,'* I whispered, repeating the provocative phrase he'd uttered earlier, in an attempt to sound more confident and provocative.

He toasted me too and knocked back the last of his wine.

But when his gaze fixed on my face again, while it still prickled over my skin, ablaze with an intense, focused desire that still disturbed me on so many levels, something crucial had been lost—his regard for me as a worthy opponent and an intelligent woman. He was looking at me now as an object of desire and contempt, not as an equal. The way all my mother's 'protectors' had always looked at her.

Anxiety and inadequacy twisted in my stomach, wrestling with the confusion and longing that was already there. I tried to dismiss the feeling of regret that he despised me now.

It was stupid to care what he thought. I wasn't here to impress him. I was here to win this game by whatever means necessary. And who was he to judge me anyway? A man who had made his fortune by ruthlessly exploiting the addictions of poor, deluded fools like my brother-in-law until they forgot about everything that mattered. And betrayed everyone who loved them.

I pushed the contempt I felt for myself and this necessary charade onto him. If I looked at it that way, Dante Allegri was as much to blame for my family's disastrous circumstances as Jason was. Maybe more so, because Jason had always been weak and easily led, unlike Allegri, who must have come out of his mother's womb with a well-developed sense of entitlement and a complete lack of compassion and empathy or how would he ever have been able to achieve what he had?

Unfortunately my growing sense of grievance against Allegri did nothing to temper the huge surge of adrenaline when he wiped his mouth with his napkin, threw it on the table and then stood and held out his hand.

'Come with me, Miss Spencer. I have something you might enjoy seeing before we resume our play.'

He towered over me. He was a tall man, at least six foot

three, and I was only a sliver over five foot four but, with his shirt sleeves rolled up and standing over me, it wasn't just his height that was intimidating. This close, I could see how toned and powerful his body was beneath the tailored shirt and trousers. All lean muscles and coiled strength, he looked like a bareknuckle fighter who would be completely merciless in his pursuit of the win.

The enormity of what I was trying to achieve—beating Allegri at his own game in his own casino—hit me with staggering force but, instead of my flight instinct kicking in, as it probably should have done, the surge of adrenaline, and the rising tide of anger, at all my family had suffered as a result of this man's cold-blooded business practices, had my fight instinct kicking in instead.

Whatever happened now, I would do everything and anything to beat this man.

I took the hand he offered and forced what I hoped was a seductive, confident smile onto my lips. 'That sounds intriguing,' I said, pleased when my voice barely quivered.

But when he folded my arm under his, tugging me close to his side—until all I could feel was the bunch and flex of his strong body next to mine and all I could smell was the clean scent of cedar soap and the devastating scent of him—my fight instinct blurred into something volatile and dangerous.

He escorted me to the mullioned window which looked out over the bay and let go of my arm, to step behind me.

'Over there,' he said as he pointed into the inky blackness over my shoulder.

'What am I looking at?' Was he about to show me his yacht? I wondered. I wanted to believe he was vain and conceited, even though all I'd seen so far was passion and purpose—and an arrogance that he had clearly earned.

But just as I became far too aware of the masculine scent

surrounding me, and the warmth of his body against the bare skin of my back, a red glow burst over the edge of the horizon, grabbing all my attention.

I gasped, shocked by the flagrant beauty of the natural light show as it spread and shimmered across the night sky, turning from red to pink to orange and myriad shades in between.

'It's beautiful,' I whispered.

I'd never seen the Northern Lights before. I didn't even know you could see them in Monaco, believing them to be a phenomenon of the Arctic Circle. My heart leapt into my throat. How had he known they would occur at this very moment? It was almost as if he'd conjured them especially for me.

I struggled to dismiss the foolish romantic thought, recognising it for what it was, a notion borne out of an overpowering physical response that I had not prepared for. But then he rested a hand on my hip and the gentle brush of his palm spread the fire in my belly through my body with the same intensity as the conflagration on the horizon.

I stood all but cocooned in his arms. I knew I should step away from him, the deep drawing sensation in my abdomen far too compelling. But the huff of breath against my ear, the intoxicating scent of soap and man, the strength of his restraint as he tensed behind me had the last of my caution flying out of the window.

We stood there together for several minutes, watching the show—and the drawing sensation in my stomach heated and spread. The mass of contradictions he stirred within me became harder and harder to explain. Why did he excite me so much? How could I enjoy standing so close to him when I knew how dangerous he was?

I shifted and turned as the lights began to fade.

His face was lit by the dying embers of the Aurora Borealis and a passion so fierce and all-consuming it terrified me. But it exhilarated me more.

It wasn't terror I felt when he brought his hand up to cup my cheek then drew his thumb down my neck in a slow glide, to settle against the rampaging pulse on my collarbone. It was longing.

'Don't look at me like that, Edie,' he murmured, using my Christian name—and the only real name I'd given him—for the first time. 'Unless you want to share my bed once the game is over.'

It was supposed to be a warning, but to my dazed mind and the pheromones hurtling through my body it sounded more like a promise.

A promise I didn't want to refuse.

I lifted shaking palms to his stubble-roughened cheeks. He clenched his jaw and tried to pull back, but I refused to let go.

Just this once, I wanted to go with my instincts and to hell with the consequences.

'Damn it,' he swore softly, but then he dragged me into his arms.

Joy burst through me—so inappropriate and yet so intoxicating—at the realisation I had snapped his cast-iron control.

He captured my lips with his. The kiss was firm and forceful, and demanding. Heat swooped into my sex and swelled in my breasts, shimmering through my body like the lights in the fiery night sky. My nipples tightened into hard aching points against the unyielding wall of his chest. My thighs trembled as his hands grasped my buttocks and drew me tight against him so I could feel the full measure of what I'd done to him. The thick outline of his erection ground against my belly.

The size and hardness shocked me, but it thrilled me more.

He wanted me as much as I wanted him. This seduction was real. We were equals.

His tongue thrust deep into my mouth in a relentless rhythm, devouring me. I opened my mouth wider, met his tongue thrust for thrust, the hunger consuming me.

But as the kiss continued, the sensations bombarding me became too strong, too overwhelming. What was happening to me? He was destroying my resistance and every ounce of my will. Why did I yearn to surrender to him?

I stopped massaging his scalp and gripped the silky waves of his hair in shaking fingers to tug his head back.

He grunted but let me go so abruptly I stumbled.

My survival instinct finally kicked in—several minutes too late—and I scrambled back, scared that I would throw myself back into that maelstrom of needs and desires if he made any attempt to kiss me again.

But he made no move towards me, his ragged breathing as tortured as my own. He swore, a guttural murmur of Italian street slang that I didn't understand, then swung away and stalked towards the window. The horizon was dark again, the dance of iridescent colours gone.

He thrust his fingers through his hair, then shoved his hands into his pockets. His broad shoulders rose and fell as he heaved out a breath, his big body silhouetted by the sprinkle of lights from the bay.

At last he turned back to me but, with his hair mussed and his movements far from smooth, he was nothing like the man who had faced me across the poker table and then the dinner table. No longer confident and controlled, and indomitable—instead he seemed wild, or barely tame, like a trapped tiger prowling the bars of its cage.

I touched trembling fingers to my lips, the soreness both devastating and invigorating. This new side to him should have scared me more but as he walked back towards me, still struggling to get a grip on the desire which continued to reverberate through my own body, I felt a giddy sense of kinship.

Was he as disturbed by the ferocity of that kiss, and how quickly it had raged out of control, as I was?

'Forgive me,' he growled when he reached me. 'That got out of hand a lot faster than I intended.'

The apology sounded gruff but sincere. And gave me an answer I didn't know how to handle. Dante Allegri, the ruthless unprincipled womaniser, was a lot easier to hate than the man before me, who seemed almost as troubled by that kiss as I was.

'Can we… Can we get back to the game?' I managed at last, surprised by my ability to string a coherent sentence together.

One eyebrow rose a fraction, but then he nodded.

'Yes,' he said.

Lifting one hand out of his pocket, he directed me to precede him into the poker salon. He made a point of not touching me again but, once we were seated at the table and he began to deal the cards, I could see he had regained his composure, and that cast-iron control.

I lifted my hole cards and examined them, but the probabilities I should be calculating as he dealt the first of the community cards and the blind betting began refused to come. My mind and every one of my senses had turned to mush.

My heart shrank in my chest as the play continued and he won the hand.

I tried to get my mind into gear during the next hand, but my judgement was off and my concentration shot. My mind and body were still reeling from the driving needs and inexplicable emotions he had ignited with a simple kiss. A kiss I had encouraged. No, a kiss I had initiated.

I wanted to weep, my panic increasing as he won the next hand. The unrequited need smouldered in the pit of my belly—the memory of his lips on mine, his hands kneading my buttocks, his tongue exploring in deep strokes—a distraction I couldn't seem to conquer…

Long before the final hand was dealt, I knew I had lost and that I had only myself to blame. Because in those giddy moments when I had yearned for Dante Allegri's kiss, then revelled in the stunning way it made me feel and then kidded myself it had devastated him too, I had become the one thing I'd always sworn I would never be… As weak and needy and gullible as my mother.

CHAPTER SIX

'TWO FIVES...' I threw my hole cards on the table next to Edie Spencer's pair of eights. Unfortunately for her, the community cards included another five. 'You lose, *bella*,' I said, grateful that the poker game was finally over.

It had taken an epic force of will and all of my expertise to keep my mind on the cards in the last hour. Ever since that damn kiss. It was a miracle I'd managed to win. After she'd broken off the embrace, I had considered throwing the game to get this part of the evening over with so I could get my hands on her again.

It had been torture, sitting in the chair and struggling to keep my head straight while my blood rushed straight back to my groin every time she worried her bottom lip with her teeth, or the soft mounds of her breasts rose and fell against the lace of her gown.

But I had forced myself to stay focused, or focused enough, to get the job done. Yes, we clearly had phenomenal chemistry, the sort of explosive sexual connection I'd never had with any other woman. And we were both going to have fun exploring it to its fullest potential. But I wasn't going to throw a game to have her—especially as I was pretty sure that's exactly why she had initiated the kiss in the first place.

But her little plan had backfired, because if I had been

struggling to keep my head straight and out of my pants after that kiss, she'd been even more distracted.

If she'd ever had a system—something I'd begun to doubt after our conversation over dinner had revealed her to be as spoilt and capricious as every other bored little rich girl who played the casinos on their daddy's dime—it had fallen apart when we'd got back to the game.

She obviously hadn't expected that kiss to go off like a rocket the way it had—which had to be why she'd called a halt to her attempted seduction so abruptly.

But as I raked in the last of her chips, I relished the surge of heat that shot straight to my groin at the thought of what the rest of the night would hold.

She hadn't said anything, and it was hard to tell how she was taking the defeat because she had her head down. But then I detected the tiny tremor running through her body. Impatience and irritation warred with my desire.

Even though I still hadn't figured out why this woman had such a turbulent effect on my usually smart libido, I wanted to take that incredible kiss to its logical conclusion. But if she was going to start crying and try to wheedle a concession out of me because I had beaten her, she could forget it. I'd won the game fair and square and I didn't trade sexual favours—however hot they promised to be—for money.

Sure, I'd had girlfriends in the past whom I'd supported. I liked to treat women I was sleeping with well. And if I was seeing someone on a regular basis I always offered them a generous allowance so they could devote their time to me and had everything they needed. I could be demanding—my lifestyle was expensive and I needed them to revolve their schedule around mine—so it seemed only fair to offer them compensation. I also always gave them a generous parting gift when the relationship reached its natural conclusion. I was a wealthy man, I considered these women friends and I didn't want anyone calling me a cheapskate, so why wouldn't I?

But I wasn't about to be emotionally manipulated by some spoilt young woman because she'd taken a chance with her daddy's money and lost. And I resented the implication that I should.

Despite all that, as Edie continued to sit there, her head bent and her shoulders starting to tremble alarmingly, a weird thing happened. I found myself wanting to take the tremor away. And not just because I had plans for the rest of the night that would become a lot less palatable if she started freaking out about the million euros of her daddy's money she'd lost.

'*Bella*, don't get too upset. I'll sub you a million so we can have a rematch some time.' It was the best I could offer without feeling like a chump. And once I said it I warmed to the idea.

Up until we'd both got distracted by that kiss, I'd enjoyed the challenge of playing with her. Our sexual attraction had added an exciting level of eroticism to the game—like high-stakes foreplay. I would enjoy playing her again, and figuring out if she actually had a system and, if so, what it was, or whether her success in the earlier part of the evening had been down to plain old dumb luck.

Instead of taking me up on the offer though, she shook her head. Still not looking at me.

My impatience and frustration spiked, along with that weird feeling of empathy.

'Look at me, *bella*.' Leaning across the table, I tucked a knuckle under her chin and nudged her face up.

What I saw though—when her emerald eyes finally met mine—was so real it shocked me to my core.

Her eyes were dry, without the self-pitying tears I had

been expecting, but also dazed and unfocused—she looked shattered. Devastated.

A stab of something ripped through my chest. And the trickle of unwanted sympathy turned into a flood.

'*Bella?* What's going on?' I said, disorientated and concerned—not just by the haunted look in her eyes, but also by my desire to take her anguish away.

Why did she look so shattered? And why the hell did I care?

'N... N... Nothing,' she stuttered, shaking her head. She stood up. 'I have to go.'

She walked past me, her back ramrod-straight, her face a deathly shade of white, her whole body consumed by tremors now.

I grasped her arm, felt the shudder of reaction. 'Don't...'

Go.

The word got trapped in my throat before I could utter it.

Grazie a Dio.

What was wrong with me? We'd kissed, once. And yeah, it had been spectacular, and unexpected. And I wanted more. But I wasn't about to beg her to stay. So I took a different tack. 'Where are you going in such a rush? Stay and have a drink,' I said, attempting to sound relaxed and persuasive.

I tugged her round to face me, disturbed by the sparkle of moisture in her eyes. I'd been expecting tears. But the sheen of distress looked genuine, something she was making every effort to contain, not use to guilt-trip me about my win.

How could she seem so fragile and breakable now, when she'd been so strong and determined earlier in the evening? And why did I still want her so much? Because her vulnerability wasn't doing a damn thing to stem the tidal wave of longing that had tortured me ever since our kiss.

Surely it was all an act? It had to be. But why couldn't I convince myself of that?

'Bella...' I cupped her cheek, brushed my thumb across the soft skin, stupidly relieved when her pulse jumped against my palm. And her eyes darkened.

She still wanted me too. I hadn't imagined that much, at least.

'It's only money,' I said, certain the cause of her distress had to be her parents' reaction. Perhaps her father would be angry. What man wouldn't be at a million-euro loss, even an indulgent father?

'You're good. Just not good enough on this occasion. But I'll give you a chance to win it back, if that's what you want.'

'Thank you. That's very generous of you,' she said.

'Then you'll stay, join me for a drink?' I hated the element of doubt in my voice. We both knew I wasn't just talking about her staying for a drink—the promise of that kiss was still snapping in the air around us.

'Yes, okay,' she said.

'Good,' I said, more relieved and excited than I should have been at her concession. I placed a light kiss on her forehead, pleased when her breathing stuttered. I forced myself not to take her lips again though, before we were both ready.

She drew away and I had to stop myself from dragging her back into my arms, the desire to stake my claim on her all but overwhelming.

She jerked her thumb over her shoulder. 'Can I go and freshen up first?'

'Of course,' I said, even though I wanted to demand she stay.

I wasn't possessive with women. And I had no idea

where the ludicrous desire not to let her out of my sight came from, so I ignored it.

But, as I watched her leave the room, the rush of blood to my groin became all but unbearable.

I poured myself a glass of expensive single malt Scotch while I waited for her, to calm my frustration and my impatience.

Walking to the window, I savoured the smoky liquor as it burned down my throat. Once she was in my bed, and I had begun to tap the heat we had ignited with that kiss, Edie Spencer would soon forget the money she'd lost. And the problem of explaining it to her father.

Hell, if we were as good together as I was anticipating, and that kiss had suggested, I could offer to support her until the fire between us burnt out. She clearly had expensive tastes, no income of her own and enjoyed the thrill of gambling with money she hadn't earned. Perhaps I could employ her as a hostess for the week-long party I was throwing at my new estate in Nice at the end of the month? Edie would be perfect for such a role, smart, beautiful and classy—and well versed in how to charm elite businessmen after her privileged upbringing. Her skill at the table might also be useful.

Of course, I might have a job on my hands persuading her to work for a living. But after her reaction tonight to losing her father's million euro stake, I didn't think it would be that hard to persuade her to take the job. I was a generous employer. Plus taming that free spirit of hers could be enjoyable for both of us.

I bolted back the last of the Scotch, finally feeling more like myself. The burn in my throat matched the warm weight in my gut—a weight which I understood now and knew would be easily resolved once Edie returned.

I glanced at my watch, surprised she was taking so long.

My cell-phone buzzed. I lifted it out of my pocket and read Joe Donnelly's text.

We've got a problem. Call me.

I sighed, tempted to ignore the request. It was four in the morning and Edie would be back soon.

But my innate professionalism took over. Joe wasn't the hysterical type, so if there was a problem he couldn't fix it must require my attention.

I clicked on the call button.

Joe picked up instantly. 'How's the game going?' he asked without preamble.

'I won ten minutes ago, why?'

Joe cursed, the Irish slang he never used unless he was rattled.

'Is Edie Spencer still with you?' he asked.

'She's freshening up,' I said, but already the hairs on the back of my neck were going haywire.

'So she's not actually in the room with you?'

'No… What's going on, Joe?' I asked, but I already knew something was very wrong, the twisting pain in my gut one I recognised from a very long time ago.

'The bank draft she paid us with—it's forged. And so is her ID. The accounting department figured it out ten minutes ago, when they noticed a shortfall in the night's takings in the casino's accounts.'

The pain sharpened, turning into the hollow ache that had crippled me as a kid. She wasn't coming back.

'The good news is we think we might have figured out who she really is.' Joe was still talking but I could barely grasp the meaning of the words, the blood rushing in my ears, the tremble of reaction in my fingers a combination of fury and something far, far worse. Helplessness.

'Who is she?' I asked, fury burning in my gut now, obliterating the distant echo of an anguish I had once been unable to control.

'Ever heard of Madeleine Trouvé?' Joe asked.

'No,' I said, resisting the urge to shout at my friend as my head began to pound. 'Is that her real name?' I said, keeping my voice low and even, although it was the opposite of how I felt. Edie Spencer had tricked me, made a fool of me. Made me relive a moment in my life I had spent a lifetime overcoming. And she would pay for that. As well as the money she'd just swindled me out of. 'We need to track her down,' I said.

Something I intended to do personally. She owed me a million euros. But I knew it wasn't just the money. My fingers clutched so hard on the whisky tumbler it shattered in my fingers.

'Madeleine Trouvé was *the* French It girl of the nineties,' Joe continued. 'Famous for the high-profile affairs she had with a string of rich, powerful and mostly married men. Seriously, you've never heard of her?' Joe asked, sounding incredulous.

'I don't have time for twenty questions,' I shouted, losing the tenuous grip I had on my temper as I wrapped a napkin around my bleeding fingers. The sting of expensive liquor in the cuts grounded me, turning the emotion churning in my belly into a cold, hard knot of anger. 'How the hell can Edie Spencer be her—the woman I just played can't be more than early twenties...'

Dewy soft skin, artless kisses, wide guileless eyes filled with passion and then devastation. How could all of that have been a lie too?

You didn't play her—she played you...

I sucked in a shattered breath, disgusted by the wave of lust that still accompanied the memory of her. The anger spiked.

'She would barely have been born in the nineties,' I finished, my voice rising as my fevered mind tried to get a grip on the sense of betrayal, the shot of confusion, tangling with the whirlwind of anger and lust still burning in my gut.

'Yeah, I know. She's not *Madeleine* Trouvé. Madeleine died in a helicopter crash four years ago with one of her lovers. Some Spanish nobleman. We think she may be the younger of Madeleine's two daughters. Edie Trouvé.'

'How sure are you?' I asked, the tangle of lust and anger and loss muted by the fierce jolt of determination. I would find Edie and teach her a lesson she wouldn't soon forget about trying to play the wrong guy.

I wasn't some spoilt, pampered, inbred aristocrat like the men her mother had obviously favoured. I had dragged myself up—literally—from the back streets of Naples. I'd run away from a series of foster families and group homes, lived on the streets as a teenager, worked like a dog in a series of dead end jobs to earn my stake, even been left beaten and bloody in an alleyway in Paris at the age of seventeen when I'd made a miscalculation on my rise to the top. No one got the better of me. And certainly not a slip of a girl with big green eyes and a sprinkle of freckles across her pert nose…

'Pretty sure,' Joe replied, thankfully interrupting the renewed wave of longing.

Which made no sense at all.

I didn't want Edie Spencer… No, Edie Trouvé. Not any more. The heat I couldn't seem to control was just the residual effect of temper and too many hours of sexual frustration. Frustration which I could see clearly now Edie had started and then stoked every chance she got. Culminating in that blasted kiss.

Basta.

What was it they said about the apple not falling far from

the tree? The girl had learned how to tempt and tantalise men from a woman who had spent a lifetime using sex, and the promise of sex, like a weapon. Her own mother.

A woman who, for all intents and purposes, was no better than my own mother.

I cut off the crippling thought, the dangerous memories.

Don't go there. These two situations are not related. Edie Trouvé means nothing to you.

'Do you know where to find her?' I gritted out the words.

'Not yet, but we're working on it,' Joe replied.

'Good,' I said as a strange kind of calm settled over me and the roaring fury in the pit of my stomach. 'Work faster. I want her found.'

CHAPTER SEVEN

'WHAT DO YOU MEAN, the bank draft I gave Allegri's cashier was fake?' I stared at Carsoni's henchman, the aptly named Brutus, my terror mixing with a bitter sense of outrage. They'd tricked me into defrauding Allegri's casino. Already I had a debt I couldn't pay, but that had been my brother-in-law's debt. This felt worse. So much worse, because this debt was on me.

I'd sat down at that poker table in good faith. I'd played and I'd lost, through my own weaknesses, my own failings. I had very little else left now but my good name. And okay, the name I'd given Allegri had been a false one, but I had never intended to cheat him.

Maybe it was foolish to care about what he thought of me. But somehow it mattered.

'You should thank me, *ma petite*,' Brutus said, the husky tone, the sleazy use of the endearment and the way his beady eyes skimmed over my figure, as they had done a million times before—every time he paid us a visit to collect payment of Carsoni's interest—made me want to vomit. 'You're already into the boss for five million euro—why add another million to the pot?'

'But Allegri will figure it out. He could have me arrested. Fraud is a crime. And then how will I pay back

Carsoni?' Weirdly, the thought of being arrested and imprisoned didn't seem as bad as having Allegri despise me.

I locked the thought away because it made no sense. I was never going to see Allegri again. What he thought of me didn't matter; it was what I thought of myself.

Up till now I'd done everything I could to honour the debts Jason had created. Maybe the path I'd chosen had been reckless and foolishly ambitious, and stemmed from a pride in my own abilities that was misplaced, to say the least; I could see that now. But I'd never meant to do something, however inadvertently, that made me a criminal.

'Allegri's not going to figure it out,' Brutus murmured. 'You used a fake ID, remember. I arranged it myself.'

They had suggested the fake ID, in case Allegri figured out my system and had me banned. And I'd gone along with it. Because I'd been naïve and desperate. Desperate enough to believe a loan shark's bullyboy.

'And Carsoni has other ideas about how you can pay him back now.'

'What?' I scrambled back as he lifted his hand to my face. The sick weight in my stomach—which had been growing ever since I had fled The Inferno early that morning or, rather, ever since Allegri had turned over his winning hand and I'd finally woken up to the terrible mistakes I had made—twisted into something mangled and ugly.

Brutus grabbed a handful of my hair and tugged me back towards him. His breath—stale with tobacco smoke—brushed my lips. I gagged and bit down on my tongue to stop myself from throwing up, my disgust now almost as huge as my terror.

He laughed. 'Stop acting surprised. Carsoni likes you. You're a pretty little thing. And he's bored, waiting for you to pay up.'

My head hurt, my scalp stinging as he dragged me

closer, close enough to bury his face against my neck. I struggled, trying to pull away from him, revulsion skittering over my skin like a plague of cockroaches.

He twisted his fist in my hair, his tongue touching my neck. 'Stop acting so high and mighty,' he murmured. 'Your mother was a highly priced whore. Carsoni will forget about the debt if you show him the proper appreciation.'

I wanted to scream, but the scream was locked in my throat. If I screamed, Jude would come to my rescue. I couldn't risk endangering her too. Jude had no idea of the threats I'd already faced from Brutus and his boss, but this was worse. The terror was so huge now, I was almost gagging on it. But I couldn't let him see that. Bullies, in my experience, were only emboldened if you showed them your fear.

I struggled in earnest. He let me go and I fell back a step.

'We're selling the house…' I pleaded. 'It's worth at least the five million we owe.' Or I hoped it was.

I had no idea where we were going to live. But we would survive. I was young and strong and a hard worker. And so was Jude. Maybe we wouldn't have Belle Rivière any more. The small chateau was the only place we had felt safe, or important in our mother's life, growing up. But however beautiful this place was—the meadows and pastures overflowing with wildflowers, the river running through the bottom of the property where we'd swum as children during those long idyllic summers, the elegance of the eighteenth-century design my mother's grandfather had built as a summer house for his ailing wife—and, however much we loved it, it was just bricks and mortar and fond memories.

My efforts to save it, my refusal to sell it as soon as Jason had incurred the debt, had only got us deeper into trouble. It was way past time I faced reality. And stopped struggling against the inevitable. Or my reality could get a whole lot worse.

The hideous truth of how much worse had my blood running cold as Brutus stepped towards me, the lecherous smirk on his face making my skin crawl.

'Maybe it'll fetch what you owe,' he said, glancing around the empty library, devoid of furniture now and books, because we'd had to sell the lot months ago to service the interest on Jason's debt. 'And maybe it won't,' he added, his gaze landing back on me. 'Either way, money isn't what the boss wants any more.'

Fury rose up like a tidal wave to cover the fear. 'Tough, because money is all he's going to get from me.'

The slap was so sudden, and so shocking, I didn't have a chance to brace.

The pain exploded in my cheekbone, snapping my head back. I slammed into the floor, rapping my elbow on the hard wood as I attempted to break my fall.

'You think?' Brutus said, the casualness of his brutality shocking me almost as much as the pain now ricocheting through my tired body as he stood over me.

I tried to slap his hands away as he grabbed my hair again, but my movements were jerky and uncoordinated, my mind entering another dimension of shock and loss and terror as he lifted me off the ground.

'Let's see how high and mighty you are once you realise what the alternative is,' he said, the calm, conversational tone striking terror into my heart.

I kicked out at him and he hit me again. Even prepared for the pain this time, the slap exploded on my cheek and released the scream I had tried to keep locked in my throat. The buzzing in my head became louder, like whirring blades.

Swish, swish, swish. As if a helicopter were landing in

the library. I thought of Dante, his eyes burning into mine, telling me he wanted me.

I could hear Jude's crying, the door rattling.

'Edie, Edie, open the door. What's happening in there?'

My dazed mind realised that Brutus had locked it when we came in here—to discuss our latest payment. The fear became huge. I kicked at his shins and he let me go. I stumbled and fell, then scrambled up, trying to run, trying to hide from those cruel fists. But the room was bare—where could I go?

I heard shouting outside, a deep voice I recognised.

He's not here... No one can save you but yourself.

'Come here.' Brutus grabbed me again, strong fingers digging into my arm hard enough to bruise.

An almighty crash startled us both. I watched the door smash inwards and fly off its hinges.

Dante Allegri strode into the room like an avenging angel, followed by his casino manager. My mind whirred like the blades of that imaginary helicopter.

Not imaginary—had Dante come to save me?

'Call the police, Joe,' he shouted, reaching us in a few strides.

You're dreaming. It's not him. Why would he come to save you?

Brutus' bruising fingers released me.

'Who the—?' The words cut off as Dante's fist connected with the henchman's jaw. Brutus's big body folded in on itself in slow motion.

I watched him drag himself up as Dante approached him. Then, like all bullies, he raced out of the door, shoving past Joseph Donnelly and my sister.

I skittered back, crouched on the floor now, as I watched my attacker run. His footfalls echoed in my aching head—which had been stuffed full of cotton wool.

Was this really happening or was I imagining it all?

The brief jolt of euphoria turned to turmoil. A part of me knew I was in shock. But as Dante walked back towards me, flexing his fingers, the knuckles bleeding, the full import of what had happened smacked into me. The fear, the confusion, the panic cracked open like an earthquake inside me. Until all that was left was the pain.

I wrapped my arms around my knees, my whole body trembling so violently I was scared I might shake myself apart.

He knelt down, that handsome face so close to me I could smell him—spicy cologne and cedar soap and man. But still I didn't believe it. Why was he here? Why had he saved me? And then I remembered. I owed him a million euros.

'Bella,' he murmured as gentle fingers touched my cheek.

I flinched, tears leaking out of my eyes. Tears I knew I shouldn't shed. Because they were tears of self-pity.

Jude appeared by my side. 'Edie…he hit you? That bastard…'

I flinched again as she cried, her sobbing making the pain in my head and my heart so much worse. I pressed my bruised face into my knees. I didn't want Dante to see me like this. Brutalised and terrified and unable to defend myself. I was so ashamed.

But I couldn't run, or hide. I hurt all over now—the pain in my face, and my elbow, and my ribs, no longer dull and indistinct but sharp and throbbing as the adrenaline of my scuffle with Brutus wore off. I was so weary, my bones felt as if they were anchored to the floor.

I shrank into myself, with some childish notion that if I couldn't see him—and the pity on his face—he wouldn't be able to see me.

'Stop crying,' Dante said to Jude, his voice soft but steely. 'And call an ambulance for your sister.'

'Already done,' Joe, the casino manager, interrupted from above me. 'Hey, colleen, come with me; your sister's going to be okay. Dante will take care of her now,' he said.

My sister's crying became muffled and distant, the casino manager's soft Irish brogue comforting her as their footsteps faded away.

Dante will take care of her now.

I stifled the pang of something agonising under my breastbone at the words. How pathetic, to want it to be true. I wasn't Dante's responsibility.

I kept my head buried in my knees and began to rock, even though each movement made the pain increase. The yearning would show on my face and I couldn't bear for him to know how much his kindness meant to me.

'Look at me, *bella*.' The gentle demand reminded me of the night before, the moment when I'd lost everything on the final turn of the cards. Or thought I'd lost everything. Why did this feel so much worse? Perhaps because, even now, I wanted to cling to the kindness he was showing me. Wanted to believe it meant something, other than the obvious thing. That he pitied the pathetic creature I had become.

I shook my head, unable to speak, still unable to look at him.

'How badly did he hurt you?' he asked and I heard the suppressed fury in his voice. 'And who was he?' he added. 'That he dared put his hands on you like that?'

I could hear more than just fury in his voice now. The underlying thread of protectiveness, and outrage, speaking to a place deep inside me which I had kept buried for so long. I couldn't allow those needs to consume me again, the way they had when I was a little girl, or they might very well destroy me.

'I'm okay,' I managed. 'Please could you leave now?'

I heard a rough breath—halfway between a sigh and a curse—and sensed him sitting on the floor beside me.

'Not going to happen, *bella*,' he said, the gruff endearment as painful as the aching pain in my cheekbone where Brutus had struck me. 'You owe me a million euro, remember.'

CHAPTER EIGHT

EDIE LIFTED HER HEAD. That had got her attention.

Rage fired through my body when I saw the red mark on her cheek where that bastard had attacked her. Who was he? A boyfriend? A husband? A pimp?

I dismissed the last possibility instantly, knowing it was beneath me and her. Just because her mother had enjoyed the protection of a string of rich men did not mean Edie was willing to sell herself to the highest bidder.

Dressed in jeans and sneakers and a T-shirt, her face devoid of make-up and her arms clasping her knees as if she were trying to hold herself together, she looked impossibly young and vulnerable. Too vulnerable.

I stifled the renewed pang of sympathy making my chest ache. The medics arriving stopped me from questioning her further about the scene I had interrupted. It was a welcome pause. I needed a chance to get a grip on the emotions rioting through me.

But as I stepped back to let them check her for a concussion and assess her injuries, it was a major struggle to remain calm and focused.

I'd come here in anger to demand she pay the money she owed me. To punish her for cheating me. And running out on me. Instead I'd walked in on a scene that had turned my fury with her—a fury which I knew now had been about a lot more than just the money—into something a great deal more complicated.

Seeing that bastard with his hands on her had ignited not just my natural rage—against any man who would treat a woman in such a way—but something more personal. As my fist had connected with the bastard's jaw and I'd felt the satisfying crunch of bone on bone it hadn't been the instinct to protect a being more vulnerable than myself, but rather the spark of something dark and possessive—a spark that had been ignited the night before, the moment I had touched my lips to hers and felt her livewire response to my kiss—that had been driving me.

I was forced to acknowledge that it was that possessive instinct too which had propelled me all the way to Northern France from Monaco this afternoon in the first place.

After all, I'd never felt the need to track down a fraudster personally before.

As she answered the paramedic's questions, I struggled to even my breathing and compose myself. The bright afternoon light flooded through dusty windows and I noticed for the first time the complete lack of furniture in the room, which must once have been some sort of library. Paint peeled from the woodwork and the faded wallpaper on the ceiling had old stains where water had leaked through from the floor above. As I studied the rundown state of the room's décor, I recalled the generally dilapidated state of the stonework on the building's exterior and the overgrown gardens which I had noticed when the helicopter had touched down outside.

The place was virtually derelict. The opposite of what I'd expected to find when I'd been obsessing about confronting Edie on her home turf in the helicopter ride from Monaco.

I'd convinced myself, after she'd run out on me and Joe

had alerted me to the fraudulent bank draft, that she was a spoilt, indulged young woman who didn't like to pay her dues. It was a picture she'd deliberately helped to create during our evening together. But the sorry state of her mother's chateau told a very different story.

The skirmish I had interrupted between her and a man twice her size had been shocking enough—and I intended to find out exactly what that was about as soon as the medics had given Edie the all-clear. But, from everything I'd seen so far, it was clear to me that, far from being spoilt brats, Edie and her sister were destitute, or close to it.

While her desperation didn't excuse her decision to enter the poker game fraudulently and then flee, I felt strangely vindicated that she was not what she had originally appeared to be. Perhaps this explained my confusing responses to her.

The young female paramedic finally finished assessing Edie. I escorted her and her colleague from the room. When we reached the door I murmured, 'How is she?'

'She's okay. No signs of concussion, just some nasty bruises,' the female paramedic told me in French as she hefted her case back onto her shoulder. 'I'll wait outside for the *gendarmes* and apprise them of her condition when they arrive so they can add it to their report.' The medic glanced over her shoulder at Edie, who sat alone on the room's window seat, staring out at the chateau's overgrown garden. 'I hope they find the bastard who did this.'

Not as much as I do.

'Will she need a follow-up appointment?' I asked, trying to keep my fury under wraps.

The woman shook her head. 'Keep an eye on her for the next few hours. If she becomes lethargic or disorientated call us back immediately. She'll have some impressive bruises tomorrow, but otherwise she should be okay.

Apart from the psychological trauma, of course,' she added darkly.

Thanking her again as she left, I returned to Edie, who looked small and frail in the empty room.

She turned towards me as I approached. 'You're still here?' she said, the wistful tone disconcerting me.

'Of course,' I replied, annoyed at the implication that I would leave without ensuring she was all right. 'I need to speak to the *gendarmes*. I intend to give them a detailed description of the man who attacked you.' I glanced at my watch. Joe had called them a good fifteen minutes ago. 'When they finally arrive.'

'Would you consider…?' She hesitated.

'Would I consider what?' I asked, the weariness in her voice and her body language making the pang worse.

'Would you consider not telling them about the bank draft? I'll pay you back every penny, I swear. But I can't do that if you press charges.'

I had absolutely no intention of informing the police about the bank draft, but I decided not to tell her that yet. There were a lot of questions I wanted answered… No, I *needed* answered. And the one million euros she owed me was the only leverage I had.

'*How* will you pay it back?' I asked, giving the empty room a pointed once-over. I didn't give a damn about the money any more, but I wanted to know exactly how bad her circumstances were. 'You don't appear to have much more left to sell.'

She blinked furiously, then looked away in a vain attempt to hide her distress. The pang sharpened in my chest. The sunlight shining through dusty glass illuminated the sheen of anguish she was trying so valiantly to contain.

'I…' She swallowed, the bold determination in the green depths reminding me of the woman who had captivated me so comprehensively at the poker table last night. 'We still own Belle Rivière,' she said. 'Even in its present state, it should fetch just about enough to pay off the mortgage we have on it and what we owe you and Carsoni.'

'Jean-Claude Carsoni?' I snapped. What the hell did that bastard have to do with this situation? 'You owe him money? How much?'

I did a quick calculation. It had to be a substantial sum because her home, however forlorn it might look, would be worth well over ten million euro.

And she'd said 'we'.

So whose debts was she paying off here? Because, from the cautious, clever way she'd played Texas Hold 'Em, right up until that kiss had distracted us both, she hadn't struck me as a problem gambler. Not only that but, after the bank draft had bounced, Joe had wired the picture taken by the security cameras when she'd entered The Inferno to all our competitors to identify her, and not one of them had ever seen or heard of her. I'd dismissed the possibility she might be a novice gambler this morning during the helicopter ride to Chantilly, because I'd been way too busy fuming about her deception.

But now I wasn't so sure. Was it possible she had little or no experience at the tables? My admiration for her—and the way she'd played—increased, which only disturbed me more.

I wasn't usually drawn to vulnerable, needy women—and under that tough cookie shell that was exactly what Edie Trouvé appeared to be—especially if she was up to her eyeballs in debt to a *bastardo* like Carsoni.

'You know Carsoni?' she said, sounding surprised.

'Enough to have him banned from operating his money-lending services anywhere near my casinos.'

Carsoni was a leech who preyed on problem gamblers

then charged them criminal levels of interest they couldn't possibly repay.

I flexed my fingers, the slight throbbing in my knuckles reminding me of the creep I'd dispatched. 'Was that one of his men, *bella*?' I asked, my concern for her increasing tenfold.

She wasn't my responsibility. Or shouldn't be. But the slow-burning anger smouldering in my gut—and the desire to take Carsoni by the throat with my bare hands and strangle him for daring to let his goons touch her—was telling me I was not going to be able to walk away from this mess. However much I might want to.

She looked out of the window again. 'I don't see how that's any of your business.'

Maybe she was right on one level, but when the sunlight caught the darkening bruise on her cheekbone, the slow burn flared into something more insistent. Capturing her stubborn chin between my thumb and forefinger, I tugged her head back towards me.

'You made it my business,' I said, 'when you came to my casino.' *And kissed me with an artless fervour I cannot forget.*

My gaze strayed to her lips, the memory of her taste, so sweet and passionate, making hunger fire through me.

Her pupils dilated and a flush flamed over her pale skin, highlighting the bruise on her cheekbone. She tugged her chin out of my grasp, but not before I'd seen the flash of heat and panic.

It is pointless to deny it, bella, *we will have to feed the hunger eventually, if we want this torture to stop.*

But the sprinkle of freckles on her nose that made her look so young, and the purpling bruise that made her look so fragile, made it clear now wasn't the time to pursue the overwhelming physical attraction we shared.

Protecting her from Carsoni and his goons and accounting for her debt to me would have to be handled first.

'I told you, I'll pay you back,' she said, but I could hear the quiver of uncertainty.

'How much do you owe Carsoni?' I asked again.

Defiance sparkled in her emerald eyes. I found it strangely pleasing. 'That's none of your…'

'Stop…' I pressed a finger to her lips, silencing her protest '…being so stubborn. And let me help. You don't want to sell your home, or you would have done it long before it came to this,' I added, letting my thumb skim under the livid bruise blossoming on her cheekbone.

'Why would you even want to help me?' she asked. 'I tried to rob you.'

Shame flickered across her face, and suddenly I knew there was more to the story of that fake bank draft than she was telling me. Had she even known the draft was fake? I wondered. If she had, why would she have stayed at the table so long—when our accounts department could discover the fraud at any time? She was an intelligent woman, however desperate she was. I didn't believe she would have put herself in that situation knowingly.

'How much do you owe Carsoni?' I demanded for the third time, letting my impatience show.

She huffed out a breath but I could see the fight leave her as her shoulders slumped. 'It was only two million to start with, but it's over five million now,' she said, the resignation making me want to do a lot more than just strangle Carsoni. The *bastardo* deserved to be hung, drawn and quartered.

'We got a loan on the property to start with, but we could never pay off enough of it. And the debt just kept getting bigger and bigger.'

I forced myself not to react. But fury tightened around my chest as the desire to eviscerate Carsoni increased.

'How was the debt incurred?' I asked, because I was convinced now that it wasn't her debt to repay.

She stared at me directly. 'Actually it was incurred in The Inferno.'

'How so?' I asked.

She sighed, resignation clear in her voice when she began to talk.

'My brother-in-law Jason and my sister Jude went on holiday to Monaco a year ago. They visited The Inferno. Jude still says she doesn't know what happened to Jason that night. He was winning at first, but then the losses started to pile up. And he wouldn't leave. Eventually he'd lost all their savings. They came back here devastated. I was angry with him, for losing everything and I told him so.' I could hear the tinge of guilt in her voice, and it annoyed me. Why was she taking responsibility for this *idiota*? But I didn't interrupt. The mention of The Inferno's involvement had unsettled me.

We made every effort to spot problem or addicted gamblers and ban them. I prided myself on running an operation where people only parted with money they could afford to lose. It seemed we would need to tighten our regulations.

'I still do not understand how your brother-in-law became indebted to Carsoni. The Inferno does not accept loans secured in his name.'

'All I know,' she continued, her voice dull and lifeless, 'is that a week later Jason got a loan from Carsoni and returned to Monaco. I suppose he didn't lose that money at The Inferno.' Her shoulders bowed as if she were carrying a ten-ton boulder on her back, probably because that is exactly what she had been doing for over a year. 'I guess he wanted to win the money back. We haven't seen or heard from him since. Carsoni turned up a week after Jason disappeared with the credit agreement Jason had signed in Jude's name.'

So the debt was her brother-in-law's and by extension her sister's… And yet she'd had no hesitation in taking it on.

Every one of my assumptions about her had been incorrect. She wasn't spoilt, lazy or a coward. Why that should make my hunger for her more acute wasn't something I wanted to think about—because it also made it more problematic.

The desire to throttle Carsoni and Edie's idiot brother-in-law was much easier to explain. I despised men who preyed on women.

'You should have told me all this when you arrived at The Inferno,' I said, frustrated at the thought that she had come to the casino, and participated in the game, primarily to win back money which had been lost, in the first instance, at my roulette table.

I had no reason to feel guilty. I ran a business—if people chose to play, they had to deal with the consequences. But the qualification wasn't doing a damn thing for the pang spreading across my breastbone and tightening around my ribs like a vice.

She glanced at me then, surprise evident on her face. 'Why would I do that? It's not your problem; it's mine.'

'It is my problem now, as there is a matter of one million euros to repay.'

She flushed. 'Once we sell the chateau I can…'

'No,' I said, startling her, as I became increasingly annoyed with her stubbornness. 'You are not selling your home. I will not allow it.'

'That's not your choice to make,' she said.

I forced myself to dial down on my frustration. She had been brought to the brink of ruin because of her brother-in-law's recklessness, and then roughed up by one of Carsoni's men. She couldn't afford to refuse my help.

But as I opened my mouth to tell her what I planned to do about this situation, I heard the *gendarmes*' sirens.

I swore softly. *About damn time.*

She looked relieved by the interruption.

We spoke to the police together, but when she was questioned about the goon who had been hitting her when I arrived she said she couldn't identify him.

I knew she was lying because she watched me as she spoke to the young *gendarme*, her eyes pleading with me not to intervene—and contradict her.

I remained silent. But only because I knew that informing the *gendarmes* of Carsoni's involvement was not the answer.

As the police left us to question her sister Jude and Joe about the incident, Edie murmured under her breath, 'Thanks, for not saying anything about Carsoni.'

I nodded.

'And for punching that creep for me,' she added. 'I should have said that sooner.'

'No thanks is necessary,' I said, biting down on my irritation at her polite, impersonal tone.

She was clearly exhausted. And I had no inclination to argue with her further.

I knew exactly how to handle a vile parasite like Carsoni. I had refrained from correcting her—and informing the police of her attacker's identity as one of Carsoni's goons—for the simple reason that I knew the police wouldn't be able to touch the money lender. And without Carsoni's help it would be impossible to track down the man who had attacked Edie.

I, on the other hand, intended to make sure both men paid for what they had done to Edie. And, unlike the police, I did not intend to play by the rules.

She pressed a hand to her forehead.

'Have you got a headache?' I asked, concerned by the deathly colour of her skin, which only made the purpling bruise on her cheek more pronounced.

'It's not too bad, considering,' she said, looking ready to keel over.

At last the police left, with promises to start a search for the attacker, who I had no doubt would be long gone by now.

I directed my attention to Jude, who still had Joe hovering over her. I'd never seen my casino manager quite so attentive with a woman before—but then Jude Trouvé was almost as beautiful as Edie. Almost. Which probably explained Joe's attentiveness. He was a man who appreciated beauty as much as I did.

'Edie needs to rest—can you keep an eye on her?' I asked Jude, who looked almost as washed out as her sister. 'The paramedics said to look out for signs of lethargy or disorientation.'

'Yes, of course.' Jude put a gentle arm around Edie's shoulder.

'I don't have time to rest,' Edie said wearily, trying to shrug off Jude's arm. 'We've got to put the house on the market—'

'There's no need to do it today,' I interrupted.

In fact there would be no need to do it at all, once my legal team had contacted Carsoni and informed him of what was going to happen next, if he wanted to stay out of prison. But she had that stubborn look in her eyes again, and I decided to humour her rather than indulge in a pointless argument that would just exhaust her more.

I fully intended to handle this situation, with or without her permission, but I needed to make sure she was being properly taken care of before I could leave.

'Mr Allegri is right, Edie.' Jude tightened her arm on her sister's shoulders before she could argue further. 'We can worry about the money again tomorrow. It's not like the problem's going to disappear if you worry about it more now.'

I said nothing as I watched her sister usher her up the stairs. Edie allowed herself to be led, the last of the fight having drained out of her. The sight of those bowed shoulders and her painful movements made it hard for me to speak round the ball of outrage in my throat.

When they reached the landing, Jude glanced over her shoulder. 'Thank you so much, Mr Allegri.' Her gaze landed on Joe and her skin flushed a becoming shade of pink. 'And you too, Mr Donnelly. I consider you both knights in shining armour. I can't thank you enough for saving Edie from that brute.'

I didn't want her thanks, any more than I had wanted Edie's. And I knew damn well I was the opposite of a knight—in or out of armour. But I nodded anyway.

'Would you be okay to see yourselves out?' she added, her request gentle but firm. I nodded again. I had a job to do before I returned to check on Edie.

As Joe and I left the chateau, it occurred to me that while Edie was the bolder of the two sisters, Jude had a quiet strength that was equally impressive.

'Jude told me that creep Carsoni is at the bottom of this,' Joe growled as we walked down the driveway towards the helicopter. 'Apparently they owe him some astronomical amount of money—and the debt just keeps increasing.'

'I know,' I said as I climbed into the cockpit of the helicopter, my fury at the whole situation flaring again. 'Rest assured, by tomorrow they will owe him nothing.'

CHAPTER NINE

I GROANED AS I rolled over in bed the following morning, awoken by the shaft of sunlight streaming through the old casement window in my bedroom. The pain in my cheekbone and my elbow though didn't hurt as much as the hollow ache in my stomach at the thought that this would be my last summer at Belle Rivière.

I crawled out of bed and walked over to the window seat where I had spent countless lazy hours reading books on everything from geometry to Gauguin to *Green Gables* in those idyllic summer months when our mother had been vivacious and happy, usually because she had a new protector. That state of bliss had never lasted very long—because rich, powerful men had a tendency to get easily bored, especially when the woman they were dating had the sort of emotional baggage my needy, insecure mother carried with her everywhere she went. But in the brief weeks and months of a new affair Jude and I had learned to be as inconspicuous and undemanding as possible, so that my mother could concentrate on the new man in her life. And stay happy. That usually meant boarding schools in England in the winter months and Belle Rivière in the summer, where we would stay with the staff while my mother gallivanted about the country on the arm of her new beau.

The boarding schools would change frequently, according to my mother's whim and what the man she was currently attached to was prepared to pay for our education. But summers in Belle Rivière had been the one constant in our lives. And it was here that I missed her the most.

My mother had been far from perfect, but on her good days she had been a force of nature that could line any dark cloud with dazzling silver sparkles. If she was here now, she would be able to take the worry away—probably with an impromptu picnic or a dress-up party—she'd never been good on finding practical solutions but she had been a master of delightful distractions. When she died, all the light and laughter was sucked out of my life and Jude's. And, however impractical it was, I would do anything for even a tiny glimmer of those dazzling sparkles right now.

I sat down and gazed out of the window at a scene I had come to love over those frenetic summers. But all I could see was the beauty I was going to lose.

The forest of oaks and pines and spruce marked the perimeter of the sixteen-acre property, the ruins of an old stone chapel in the distance overgrown with wild roses. A carpet of poppies added a splash of vibrant red to the intense greens of the meadow leading down to the river. I prised open the window latch, forced open the swollen frame and breathed in the perfume of wild flowers and pine sap I had come to adore. I could hear the musical tinkle of the river in the distance which wound its way along the bottom of the meadow shielded by the valley of trees and reminded me of my mother's laughter—bright and bubbly and so beguiling.

I swallowed heavily. How was I going to survive without this oasis in my life? After losing my mother, I wasn't sure I could bear to lose this too.

I squeezed my fingers to the bridge of my nose and then wiped away the tear that slid over my sore cheek.

'Edie, at last you're up.'

I turned and winced, my neck muscles protesting at the sudden movement. Jude stood in the doorway, grinning.

'Hi,' I grumbled, massaging the stiffness.

'How are you feeling?' she asked as she rushed across the room, her voice a mixture of concern and something that sounded weirdly like excitement.

'I'm okay,' I said, determined not to worry her any more than I had already. 'I just wish…' I blinked. *Don't cry—it'll only make this situation worse.* 'I wish I could have found a way for us to keep Belle Rivière.'

If only I could burrow into a ball in the centre of my bed and make all the worries disappear, the way I'd sometimes had to do as a little girl, when I could hear my mother's crying, or the feral sounds of lovemaking from her room next door, which had always confused and frightened me.

Jude plopped herself opposite me and took my hand in hers. 'I think we can save Belle Rivière after all, because I've got some news.'

'What news?' I said, wanting to believe her but unable to shift the lump of failure and old grief wedged in my throat.

'Incredible, incredible news,' Jude said, grasping my hands and enjoying the suspense. 'Dante Allegri just called—he's got Carsoni to cancel the debt. We don't owe that bastard another cent.'

'He's…? What?' That got my attention. I stared at her blankly, forcing myself to quash the leap of pure joy in my heart. A hope dashed was so much harder to bear than no hope at all. 'But… How did he manage that?'

'I have no idea,' she said, her smile so bright it hurt my eyes. 'I didn't ask, because I really don't care. All I care about is that no one ever hurts you like that again. If we get to keep Belle Rivière that's even better.' She clasped my arms, but the hope starting to bloom under my breastbone meant I couldn't even feel the bruises. 'But you're the only thing I really care about,' she said. 'I should never have let you take the risks you did.' She glanced around the room—the faded curtains, the moth-eaten rug, the worn bed sheets. 'I love this place too, but nothing's more important to me than you, Edie.'

'He must have paid him off,' I said, the leap of joy in my heart joined by that disturbing feeling of connection I'd tried so hard to ignore the afternoon before—when Allegri had punched Brutus for me. 'It's the only thing that makes any sense.'

'Blimey, do you really think so?' Jude said, her eyes popping wide. 'But we owed Carsoni over five million euros by the last estimate.'

'I know,' I said, my stomach churning with shock.

Nobody had ever done anything like that for me before. But why would he?

The urgency and hunger in his kiss blasted into my memory—and made the churning in my stomach become hot and languid. Was it possible…?

'He must like you an awful lot…' Jude said, her thoughts straying into the same uncharted territory as mine. 'But then, he did beat up Brutus for you.'

I forced myself to contain the leap of excitement at the memory of that punch.

Get a clue, Edie. Dante Allegri can have any woman he wants. For goodness' sake, the man dates supermodels. Why would he want you?

I pressed trembling fingers to my lips, the memory of his tongue commanding the inside of my mouth in greedy strokes sending my senses reeling.

Okay, he had wanted me as much as I had wanted him, during that searing kiss. But even I knew the promise of that kiss wasn't worth five million euros. I was still a virgin. I had zero experience. Then again, he didn't know that.

'Do you think…?' Jude stared at me, her mind still heading in the same insane direction as mine. 'Do you think he'll expect you to become his mistress?'

'I don't know,' I said, not nearly as horrified at the prospect as I probably ought to be.

Inappropriate and unbidden heat flushed through my system. The thought of sleeping with Carsoni for money had disgusted me, but the thought of taking that kiss to its logical conclusion with Allegri didn't disgust me at all. In fact, at the moment the only thing that was really worrying me was the thought that once he found out I was a virgin, and I didn't know the first thing about pleasuring a man, he might ask for his five million euros back.

Which was probably very bad of me. After all, agreeing to become Allegri's mistress because he'd paid off a five-million-euro debt for me would compromise me, the way my mother had always been compromised. Really, I ought to feel trapped and humiliated. But I couldn't seem to muster the required shame or indignation. At all.

Because the prospect of being free of debt was almost as intoxicating as the memory of that turbo-charged kiss… And where it might lead.

'Well, I guess we're going to find out,' Jude said, looking sheepish. 'Because he's coming over later today to check up on you.'

My heartbeat bumped my throat, threatening to gag me, while the heat sunk deep into my abdomen.

I'd entered the game at Allegri's casino and lost—precisely because I had been determined to prove I was not as needy as my mother. But as the heat spread through me, softening my thigh muscles and dampening my panties at the thought of what Dante might want from me, I wasn't even sure of that any more.

CHAPTER TEN

'I CAN'T THANK you enough for helping us, Mr Allegri. My sister and I are completely beholden to you. I'm more than willing to show you my gratitude in any way you think is appropriate. Even though I'm aware that five million euros is a lot more than my gratitude is worth.'

'What five million euros are you talking about, *bella*?' I asked, trying to keep a grip on my temper as my gaze roamed over the livid bruise on Edie Trouvé's cheek, which had spread into a dark circle under her eye overnight.

What insanity was this now? And was there no end of ways this woman could stir both my desire and my exasperation?

She stood before me in the furniture-less room where she had been attacked the day before, sporting the marks that Brutus Severin had inflicted, looking as if a strong wind would blow her down. But, despite her obvious fragility, she seemed not to realise how vulnerable she was, her face open and eager and full of hope, as if I were some kind of saviour. Nothing could be further from the truth.

'Didn't you pay Carsoni the money we owe him?' she asked. 'To get him to cancel the debt?'

'No, I did not.'

She frowned, clearly confused. 'But then, how did you get him to cancel it?'

My exasperation increased at the realisation that my hunger for her had not abated in the least, despite her obvious naiveté.

'I didn't get him to cancel the loan; my legal team did,' I said. 'The credit agreement your brother-in-law signed was invalid.' Or, rather, Carsoni had been persuaded that trying to enforce it would cost him more than the debt was worth, not just in money but also in a lethal blow to what was left of his reputation on the Côte D'Azur. 'Carsoni was only too happy to forego the debt once he realised he would be meeting the might of the Allegri Corporation in court—instead of two penniless women—if he chose to collect any more money from you.'

I had also had my lawyer inform him that he and his organisation would be the subject of a criminal investigation if I chose to inform the police who had employed Severin.

'I… Oh.' She sounded more disconcerted than pleased by this revelation. 'So you didn't pay him five million euros on our behalf?' she asked again.

'No, I most certainly did not.'

'I see. Well, that's good. That's very good.' A blush flared across her chest.

She looked disconcerted, even a little deflated, the vivid blush riding her collarbone and seeping into her cheeks.

It occurred to me she had painted herself into an interesting corner with the suggestion I had paid off Carsoni. A corner I couldn't resist shining a light into.

'What kind of gratitude did you have in mind, *bella*?' I asked. The blush illuminated the freckles on her nose.

'I… Can you forget I said that?' she said.

'No, I think not,' I said, not about to let her off so easily. Seeing her rattled felt like payback. Because she had done nothing but rattle me ever since I had first laid eyes on her. 'I'm just wondering what kind of gratitude would be worth five million euros?'

'It doesn't matter,' she said, busy avoiding eye contact.

My lips quirked. Damn, but she was even cuter when she was mortified.

'Five million euros is a lot of money,' I mused. 'I would expect something very exceptional for that amount,' I added, openly teasing her now.

The strange thought that she would be worth every cent of that amount hit me unawares though, as she raised her head and stared at me.

Her soft skin was flushed with embarrassed heat but her eyes sparkled with a strength of character that reminded me of a battle-weary Valkyrie.

Edie Trouvé might be that very rare thing, a woman as honest and open as she was fearless.

Desire flushed through my system.

What would it be like to have such a woman in my bed, surrendering herself to pleasure?

The stab of longing at the thought disturbed me on a level so visceral, my amusement at the situation faded.

Edie Trouvé wasn't fearless; she was desperate. And on one level she had just insulted me, by offering me her 'gratitude' in payment for five million euros. There was nothing honest or open about what she'd implied. Sex was always a transaction, just like everything else in life, but all she'd done was prove that point.

I'd learnt at a very young age that needs and desires only made you weak. I'd made my fortune, forged a future for myself alone, without relying on or having to trust anyone, knowing that no one gave anything freely. There was always a price, and Edie's offer was no different.

'You're mocking me,' she said, the sparkle of excitement gone from her eyes. 'But I do want to thank you, Mr

Allegri, for contacting Carsoni and making this happen. If you let me know what the legal fees are I'll endeavour to repay you that.'

I should have been vindicated by her surrender. But somehow the defeated tone had the exact opposite effect.

Exasperation gave way to annoyance. 'My legal team are on a retainer, so there are no additional fees for this work.'

She nodded. 'Then it's just the matter of repaying the million euros I owe you.'

'That debt is erased too,' I said curtly.

'Are you sure?' she said.

'Tell me honestly,' I said. 'Did you know the bank draft was fraudulent?'

She paused for a moment and then shook her head. 'But I still lost the money at the table. So surely I still owe it to you.'

I nodded. 'Yes, but unfortunately it's very clear you cannot afford to repay it.'

The flush of arousal, the rapid rise and fall of her breathing and the nipples visible against the worn cotton of her T-shirt, were making it hard for me to concentrate on the conversation.

The urge to take her in my arms and kiss that concerned look off her face was not something I could pursue while she was still bruised from yesterday's assault. I had come here with an entirely different purpose. One I needed to focus on now, before I did something I might later regret.

I needed time to properly assess my attraction to this woman. Because, in light of her current circumstances, it made even less sense than it had two nights ago, when I'd believed her to be the spoilt daughter of a rich man.

Pint-sized Valkyries weren't my type any more than spoilt little rich girls.

But I had mulled over her situation and done some Internet research on her and her family during the night I'd spent in a nearby hotel and had decided that offering her a position as part of my team for the upcoming house party at my estate on the Côte D'Azur made even more sense now than before.

She might currently be destitute, but her family had an aristocratic lineage that could be traced back to the Huguenots and the highest echelons of British high society. She was the bastard issue of her mother's affair with the married younger son of a British duke. Her great-grandfather had been a French count and one of her grandfathers that British duke. Maybe her father and her father's family had never acknowledged her. But that blue blood still ran through her veins—while mine was as red and wild as the poppies that grew in abundance in the fields outside the house.

She had, no doubt, gone to the best schools, while I had learned my lessons on the back streets of Naples, scrapping and struggling for every single bite. And, while no one knew the full degradation of my heritage, everyone knew I had come from nothing. I was a gambler, a self-made billionaire, and while I had always been proud of what I had achieved, having her as part of my team at this event would give me a status I could use—a bankable commodity which I was more than happy to pay for.

And her skills at the table would be invaluable if used properly.

In some ways, our circumstances weren't all that dissimilar. She was illegitimate too, and had been at the mercy of forces beyond her control. Like me, she had worked hard to rise above her circumstances, the way I had worked hard to rise above my station and erase the circumstances of my birth.

But my admiration for her ended there. And giving her a chance didn't have to mean anything other than that. As long as she understood that I was not a charitable man, and I didn't do anything out of the goodness of my heart—because I really didn't have a heart. After all, I had been careful to cut it out ever since…

I shut off the thought, the shaft of memory not something I wished to revisit.

The two situations were not the same. I had been a child then. I was a man now. A man who had made himself invulnerable to pain.

'Your sister told me exactly how deep your financial troubles go,' I said. 'I have a possible solution.'

'What is it?' she said, desperation plain on her face.

'Would you consider working for me?' I asked.

'You're… You're offering me a job?'

She sounded so surprised, I found my lips curving in amusement again.

'As it happens, I am hosting an event at my new estate near Nice at the end of the month. I could use your skills as part of the team I'm putting together.'

'What exactly do you need me to do?' she said, her eagerness a sop to my ego.

'The guests I am inviting are some of the world's most powerful businessmen and women.' I outlined the job. 'They have all shown an interest in investing in the expansion of the Allegri brand. The event is a way of assessing their suitability as investors. As part of the week, I will be offering some recreational poker events. These people are highly competitive and they enjoy games of chance. What they don't know is that how they play poker tells me a great deal more about their personalities and their business acumen—and whether we will be compatible—than a simple profit and loss portfolio of their companies. But I find that successful people, no matter how competitive they are, are also smart enough to know that they cannot best me at a poker table. So I need someone who does not intimidate them, but who can observe how they play and make those assessments for me.' I kept my eyes on her reaction, surprised myself by how much I wanted her to say yes.

My attraction to her might be unexpected, but I had spent a lifetime living by my wits and never doubting my instincts. When I had originally considered giving her a hosting position I'd been aware of the possible fringe benefits for both of us and I didn't see why that should change. She had made it very clear she was more than happy to blur the lines between employer and lover, and all her responses made it equally clear she desired me as much as I desired her.

'I'll pay you four thousand euros for the fortnight,' I said, to make her position clear. This was a genuine job, and a job she would be very good at. 'Joe can brief you on each of the participants—and what I need to know about them. If you do a good enough job, and your skills prove as useful as I'm expecting them to be, I would consider offering you a probationary position.'

She blinked several times, her skin now flushed a dark pink. But didn't say anything.

'So do you want the job?' I asked, letting my impatience show, annoyed by the strange feeling of anticipation. Why should it matter to me if she declined my offer?

'Yes, yes,' she said. 'I'll take the job. And thank you.'

Triumph surged up my chest, which seemed out of proportion to what I had actually achieved. Of course she'd said yes—why on earth would I doubt it? And why should I even care that much?

She tugged at her lip. Desire bloomed in my groin and I had my answer. My eagerness to have her in my employ was about physical desire and exceptional chemistry, nothing more or less.

I pulled a card out of my back pocket and handed it to Edie. 'Joe will contact you with all the necessary details of your employment in a couple of days,' I said. 'If you need to contact me directly, my personal number is on the card.'

She took the card and nodded. Then the strangest thing happened—the line of her lips tipped up on one side. The smile was tentative and shy and self-deprecating, but it lit her eyes, giving them a glow which highlighted the shards of gold in the emerald green of her irises.

The jolt hit my chest unawares as it occurred to me I'd never seen her smile before. It only made her beauty rarer and more exquisite.

She ran her thumb over the card, the sheen of moisture in those stunning eyes making the jolt twist sharply.

'Thank you, Mr Allegri—for everything,' she said, her gratitude genuine and heartfelt and all the more disturbing for it. 'I won't disappoint you, I swear.'

'Then start by calling me Dante,' I said.

'Thank you, Dante,' she said.

I turned and left but as I climbed into my car and drove off the estate the jolt refused to go away, forcing me to consider the possibility that my attraction to Edie Trouvé went beyond the physical… Which would not be good at all.

CHAPTER ELEVEN

AS THE HELICOPTER touched down on the clifftop heliport, I was sure my eyes were literally popping out of their sockets at the sight before me.

Belle Rivière was beautiful, but it had none of the sheer grandeur and elegance of Dante Allegri's estate on the Côte D'Azur. Over ten acres of manicured gardens, arranged in terraces leading down to the sea on three sides, the grounds were peppered with statues and follies, waterfalls and lavish ponds as well as a huge marble swimming pool at the back of the villa with steps leading down to a dock and one of the estate's three private beaches.

Guest houses were nestled among the gardens, but the house itself stood proud as the centrepiece. I estimated the chateau had to have at least twenty or thirty bedrooms as the helicopter circled the building. A summer house originally built for a Portuguese prince, the mansion, with its rococo flourishes, elegant walkways, Belle Époque frontage and lavish plasterwork, had been described by Joseph Donnelly as a villa, but that description seemed far too modest for the palace below me.

I had known Dante Allegri was a rich man, but I'd never really considered how rich.

Two members of staff appeared at the heliport to greet

me as I stepped down from the aircraft. Joseph had seen me off in Monaco less than twenty minutes ago.

I had spent the last three days with him and the casino staff being briefed on the guests who would begin arriving in a few days for Dante Allegri's house party. I'd taken copious notes on the names and faces, the businesses they owned and what their preferences were, and how I should address them—I'd also researched their finances and how they'd made their money, so I could observe their play and assess their attitudes to risk with more context.

I hadn't seen Allegri while I was staying in the apartment assigned to me at the casino, and I had been grateful for that. I needed as much time as possible to calm my nerves and get a grip on my instinctive reaction to him before I saw him again.

I wanted to make a good impression. I needed to earn the probationary position he'd mentioned, if I was going to have any chance of salvaging not just my pride, but my family's finances and Belle Rivière. Allegri's actions had freed us from Carsoni's threats and the crippling debts, but we still had a sizeable mortgage on the estate and the house itself was rundown and unfurnished. Jude had suggested we turn it into a bed and breakfast inn, so we could make it self-sufficient, but for that we would need to invest in it. And a new job with good prospects could provide the capital we so desperately needed if Dante Allegri offered it to me.

Allegri... No, Dante, I corrected myself, as my skin heated. Dante had given me an opportunity—an opportunity I wanted to make the most of.

Thank goodness he didn't know my experience of these sorts of high society events was precisely zero. My mother had been shunned by polite society in both the UK and France—and my only experience of it was the years

I'd spent observing the behaviour of the daughters of the wealthy in boarding school and, more recently, the jobs I'd had cleaning the houses of the rich and privileged.

But, while I might not have a profile in society, I did understand numbers. And probabilities. Joseph Donnelly had told me Dante was a man who preferred cold hard facts. If I could give him a numerical breakdown of exactly how well each person played—what risks they took and didn't take, the bets they made and the bets they won, how often they bluffed, et cetera—I would be able to amass a wealth of data which he could use to his advantage. I'd already worked out several formulas to assist me in compiling the data.

More than anything, I wanted to impress upon him that he hadn't made a mistake in giving me this chance. Which meant not getting ideas above my station, as I had that excruciating morning at Belle Rivière, about what he did and didn't want from me.

'Miss Trouvé, welcome to La Villa Paradis. My name is Collette; I am Mr Allegri's villa manager,' an older woman greeted me in perfect English, before directing a young bellboy to take my carry-on bag. 'Pascal will take your belongings to the guest house Mr Allegri has assigned to you. I hope your flight wasn't too tiring?'

'Not at all,' I said. The flight had been just one more eye-popping experience. I'd never travelled in a helicopter before. 'It was perfect,' I said.

Collette sent me a warm smile. 'Good, then let me show you to your guest villa. I have arranged for a light lunch to be served to you there, but if there is anything else you require just let me know.'

'Thank you.' I nodded, disconcerted by the offer and her manner. I was Dante's employee too, not a guest.

'I thought you might like to rest for an hour before meeting with the stylist,' she added. 'So I have pushed the appointment back until three o'clock, if that is okay?'

'Yes, but… What stylist?' I asked, even more disconcerted.

'Mr Allegri has hired Nina Saint Jus of La Roche to assemble your look,' she said, naming a Parisian designer and fashion house so famous even I'd heard of them.

'My look?' I repeated dully, feeling the blush warm my cheekbones.

Apart from the second-hand ball gown I'd worn to the casino the night I'd first met Dante, my wardrobe wasn't exactly illustrious, being a collection of jeans and T-shirts in various states of disrepair. But Joseph had already arranged an advance on my salary for the event, and I'd managed to find some bargains online that I had hoped would ensure I didn't look like a waif and stray Dante had dragged in off the street.

I knew I needed to look the part, that dress was important. But a stylist? And one of Nina Saint Jus's pedigree? How could I possibly afford to pay for this wardrobe? It would probably cost more than my entire salary.

'Mr Allegri has not mentioned this to you?' Collette asked with a benevolent smile on her face, as if she wasn't the least bit surprised.

'No, he hasn't.'

She sighed and rolled her eyes heavenward. 'Men!' she said and sent me a conspiratorial grin that downgraded my panic a notch. She patted my hand as she led me down a path shaded by palm trees, the flower beds choked with an array of lilies and roses that added a heavy perfume to the fresh sea air. 'Mr Allegri is arriving after lunch,' she said helpfully. 'He has requested that you meet him for dinner after your fitting; you will be able to talk to him then.'

Far from downgrading my panic, Collette's casual comment had it swelling into a ball—and head-butting my tonsils.

* * *

Ten hours later, as I was escorted through the mansion's east ballroom and up a staircase to a mezzanine level, worry sat like a boulder wedged in my solar plexus.

I had wanted to make the best possible impression today. But the fitting hadn't gone well. While I had been trying to keep the price down, the stylist and her three assistants had insisted on discarding all the clothes I had brought with me and selecting a whole new wardrobe.

For tonight, I was dressed in a fire-red satin body-con dress picked by the designer from her *prêt a porter* collection. My usually unruly hair was pinned up in a waterfall of curls that draped down my back, my make-up had been professionally done, and it had all been achieved by a team of beauty stylists who had arrived at my villa an hour before my dinner date with Dante.

The expensive satin caressed my skin as I walked. The dress was absolutely exquisite, more beautiful, and a lot more expensive, than anything I'd ever worn before in my life. The designer had referred to it as a simple cocktail dress, while taking my measurements to design a series of more formal gowns for the 'entertainments' Dante had planned for the week ahead.

To say all this activity had intimidated me would be putting it mildly.

What entertainments? I wondered.

As I walked along the balcony that skirted the ballroom, the heeled sandals I was wearing were muffled by the silk carpeting.

The mansion's grand décor—the modern art that lined the walls, the ornate plasterwork and elegant lighting—did nothing to calm my jangling nerves.

I didn't feel like me any more. When I had looked in the mirror after the styling I hadn't recognised myself.

I would have to tell Dante the truth at dinner. The truth I had hoped to keep hidden. That I really didn't fit into this world. Into his world. That I could easily make a catastrophic mess of the job he'd given me, say something gauche or inappropriate, address someone the wrong way. That it was highly likely some of the guests might have known my mother, or certainly knew of her notoriety. And that I couldn't possibly afford this wardrobe.

My escort, a young man called Gaston with a friendly smile, opened a large door and I stepped into a room that was easily the size of the whole of Belle Rivière's ground floor. Dante was standing on the other end of the huge banqueting hall, silhouetted against a view of the villa's lavish gardens, currently lit by a series of nightlights. The long table which took up most of the space was set at the far end for two people with antique crystal and fine china.

Were we eating alone tonight?

'*Bon appétit*, Mademoiselle Trouvé.' Gaston bowed and left, closing the door behind him before I had a chance to thank him.

My inadequacy started to strangle me, but it was joined by the pulsing deep in my abdomen when Dante turned. He watched me but made no move towards me, so I was forced to walk to him.

'Hi.' My greeting came out on a helium squeak worthy of Minnie Mouse. I cleared my throat, mortified now as well as nervous.

Dante's lips quirked in that knowing smile which only unnerved me more.

His gaze burned down my dress. The silky satin rubbed my sensitised skin like sandpaper.

'I see Nina has done the job I paid her for,' he said. 'You look exquisite, *bella*.'

His voice reverberated through me, making the liquid tug in my abdomen sink into my sex.

'Thank you,' I said, then bit into my bottom lip.

Tell him now, you ninny.

'There is a problem,' he said, and I realised he had noticed my nervousness. 'You don't like the dress?'

'No, I love it,' I said. 'It's just…'

'Just what?' he prompted.

'I can't afford it,' I said. 'Any of it.'

He chuckled. 'I guess it's a good thing I'm paying for it then.'

'But…' My eyes widened again. I had to look like a rabbit in the headlights by now, but I couldn't help it. I was totally overwhelmed. 'Really?'

His lips crinkled in a wry smile. The way they had when he'd teased me before, after I'd made that daft suggestion about showing him five million euros' worth of gratitude.

'Of course, I need you to look the part, Edie. Some people will assume you're my mistress.'

'They will?' The heat flared in my cheeks.

'Is that a problem?' The muscle in his jaw tensed and I had the horrible thought that I might have insulted him with my shocked reaction.

'No, not at all. It's… I just didn't expect you to pay for my clothing. As well as the generous salary you're paying me.'

The muscle relaxed and his smile returned. 'It's all part of the job, *bella*. If you really want to, you can always return the clothes to me once the event is over. But I doubt they will fit me.'

I laughed, and his smile widened.

He stepped closer and his thumb skimmed my cheek. 'Has the bruise healed? Or is that the work of a good make-up artist?'

Something shimmered through me, more than the heat. I tried to pull it back. His concern was nothing out of the ordinary. He was just being a conscientious employer. The only reason I was taking it so much to heart was that I'd never had a man look at me like that before, as if he actually cared that I had been hurt.

'Yes, it's better, thanks,' I said.

'I'm glad,' he murmured. The something shimmered through me again. He dropped his hand—and I felt a strange sense of loss. Holding out his arm, he indicated the table behind us as two serving staff entered the room. 'Let's sit down,' he said. 'This is a working dinner. We have much to discuss about next week.'

My heart lurched into my throat as he seated me and the waiters set out a selection of delicate salads, fresh bread and charcuterie for our starters.

I needed to come clean about my qualifications for this job, or rather the lack of them, I told myself. My panic attack over the clothes was proof of that.

He poured me a glass of wine and I gulped it down as he served me from the terrines on the table.

'Mr Allegri, there's something I…' I began.

'Call me, Dante,' he said. 'You are part of my team, not a waitress.'

I cleared my throat, the colour flushing through my system at the intimacy in the look he sent me. 'Dante, I'm not sure I'm who you think I am.'

'How so?' he asked, leaning back in his chair to sip his wine.

The colour rose to my hairline under that assessing gaze.

I'd never been ashamed of my background. I was illegitimate—I'd never met my father; in fact he'd never even acknowledged me or my sister. Because we'd been the product of an extra-marital affair. But, despite that, I'd never been ashamed of my mother's choices.

She'd been reckless and irresponsible and selfish in a lot of ways, and careless—especially with other women's husbands—but she'd also been loving and vivacious. And she had also been notorious, her exploits, her affairs, her lack of decorum or compunction documented in minute detail and found wanting in the tabloid press. She'd tried to shield us from that as children. But I'd heard all the whispers about her behaviour at the boarding schools I'd attended. That she was a marriage-wrecker, a slut, a whore. I'd got into enough fights over the years defending her honour, even though I knew in some ways she didn't have any. The one time I'd confronted her about one of her 'protectors' when the story had hit the tabloids that she had broken up the marriage of a famous actor—and the girls at school had made my and Jude's life a misery—she had simply laughed and said, 'If his wife wanted to keep him, she should have made more of an effort to entertain him.'

But, here and now, as I sat in front of Dante, it was hard for me to explain my upbringing without wishing it could be different.

'I think you may have got the impression because of Belle Rivière…' I swallowed, trying to alleviate the dryness in my throat '…and my background, that I'm an aristocrat and I know the workings of high society. I don't.'

He didn't seem surprised by this revelation. 'You are the granddaughter of a British duke—is this not true?'

My ribs felt as if they were squeezing my lungs. So he *had* heard the rumours. The few bites of salad I had eaten coalesced in the pit of my stomach.

'My mother always maintained as much,' I said. 'But I never met him or my father. And our father certainly never acknowledged us.' I tried to sound flippant; the circumstances of my birth had never been important to me before. Why would they? My father had chosen not to be a part of my life. But, for the first time ever, instead of feeling belligerent and indifferent about the man who had sired me, I actually wished I could claim the pedigree Dante clearly believed I had.

I didn't want to lose this job, and it wasn't about the money any more. This was the first chance I'd ever had to prove myself. And then there was the thought of being able to spend a whole ten days in his company. I might as well admit it, after his rescue a week ago and the way he had swooped in to give my sister and me a way out of our problems, not to mention the memory of that kiss, I had a massive crush on him. When he'd said that some people might consider me to be his mistress, I'd had the weirdest reaction. Not embarrassment or humiliation, but excitement and pride.

'I was educated in private schools,' I continued, because he was still watching me with that assessing gaze, not giving away his feelings about my revelations. 'But I've never been to an event like the one you're hosting here,' I finished.

His eyes narrowed and the muscle in his jaw tensed again, but I couldn't tell whether he was angry or disappointed with this information.

'Why are you telling me this?' he said at last.

The question confused me. Wasn't it obvious? 'Because I don't want to disappoint you,' I said, forcing myself to admit it. 'Although I didn't recognise any of the names on the guest list…' *Thank God.* 'Some of your guests may still have known my mother, and they may well know *of* me, that I'm…' I breathed in and looked out into the night, not able to look into his eyes any more. It was hard to say the word, because I had always been sure to make certain it did not define me, but I knew I had to be honest with him because it might very well define me now and my ability to do the job he'd given me. He'd bought me an incredible wardrobe, he'd put me up in one of the villa's guest houses, he was giving me a four-figure salary for two weeks' work and treating me with respect—as if I were more than an employee. He was even happy to have people believe we were dating. He'd shown a faith in me that no other man had ever shown, not even my own father—especially my own father—but I didn't want to take what he was offering under false pretences, especially as it might have an adverse effect on what he wanted to achieve here. Or that would make me as complicit as my mother in the many, many marriages she'd destroyed.

'That you're what?' he prodded, forcing me to bring my gaze back to his.

'That I'm a bastard,' I finally managed, pushing out the hateful word on a harsh breath. 'Mr Donnelly said one of the purposes of this event and the new expansion is to increase the public profile of your company and to give the Allegri brand additional status and respect.' I hurried on as his expression remained tense and shadowed. I had angered him with this revelation, I could see that now, even though he was making an effort not to show it. My hopes shattered. He would fire me, of course he would—what had made me think that I could hide who I really was, even for a second?

'I don't want to mess that up with my presence, or tarnish your company's brand, however inadvertently.'

CHAPTER TWELVE

I SAT STUNNED, not just by Edie's revelation—which, of course, was not news to me at all—but by the honesty and openness and genuine anguish on her face as she related her background to me. I gritted my teeth, trying hard not to reveal my reaction. And trying even harder not to feel it.

But, despite my best efforts, the all-consuming anger—towards the bastards who had ever made her think the circumstances of her birth diminished her—was followed by an even more disturbing sense of connection—at the realisation that she had once been subjected to the same petty prejudices and insults, the same cruel judgements that I had suffered so often as a boy.

She pressed her napkin down on the table and stood. 'I should leave,' she said.

Wait... What?

I got up and walked round the table to grab her before she could run out on me again. 'Where are you going?' I asked.

'Don't you want me to go?'

'Bella...' I tried, but I couldn't seem to stem the sympathy that overwhelmed me at the sight of her distress. 'Why would you think that?'

'I've just told you my mother was a...' She swallowed and I could see her struggle with the ugly word she had no doubt had levelled at her a hundred times. 'She was notorious, Dante. I don't want to…'

'Shh…' I pressed a finger to her lips. 'My mother was a street whore in Naples, Edie,' I said, breaking a silence I had kept since I was a child. 'She picked up men for pennies, screwed them in alleyways. Or brought them back to the room where we lived. My earliest memory is hearing the sounds of sexual intercourse from my crib.'

Shock widened her eyes, but I couldn't seem to stop myself from exorcising the bitter truth. Stupid that I should feel safe giving her this information. I hardly knew her, but something about the way she had confided in me, not to gain my pity or my empathy but simply to protect my company's reputation, touched a part of me I thought was incapable of being touched.

'Do you really think whatever your mother did or didn't do with the men in her life could be worse than that?'

I cupped her cheek, the softness of her skin, the brutal flush igniting her cheeks making me want to capture her mouth again and devour it.

She wasn't innocent—how could she be with a background like hers? She had grown up in the school of hard knocks, just like I had. Maybe her life had had the cushion of gentility that mine had comprehensively lacked, but we had both suffered, thanks to the weaknesses—and arbitrary prejudices—of others. It connected us in a way I might not like, but I could no longer fail to acknowledge.

'I'm so sorry, Dante,' she said, covering my hand with hers. The consoling words and the warmth in her eyes confused me—who exactly was comforting whom here? 'That must have been so traumatic for you as a young boy,' she added.

I drew my hand away, appalled by her pity, but appalled

more by the way it made me feel. Not angry, or even irritated, but moved.

'And for your mother—what a terrible life for her too,' she added, and I recoiled.

Was she serious? I had hated my mother for so long—the life she had given me, the way she had discarded me like so much rubbish, I couldn't quite comprehend what Edie was saying. I didn't want her pity, but I couldn't even understand her pity for the woman who had given birth to me.

'It was a very long time ago, *bella*,' I said, forcing an indifference into my tone that I didn't feel. I had exposed myself by confiding the details of my childhood. Why the hell had I done that? Perhaps because I wanted this woman more than I had ever wanted any woman. 'My childhood gave me the tools to become the man I am today.'

'I understand,' she said, but the sympathy still shone in her eyes. And I knew she didn't understand.

I had meant that my childhood had made me ruthless and driven, prepared to do just about anything to get away from where I had started to arrive at where I was now.

'You've worked so hard for your business,' she continued. 'But that's why I wanted you to know about...'

'I already knew,' I said, to cut off her illogical confession and the way it was making me feel. The connection I had felt to her was not something I should encourage, so why had I, with that ill-advised confession about my background?

'Bella,' I added, 'I did an Internet search on your background before I hired you.' I could see I'd surprised her, so I continued. 'Your social connections or the lack of them are of no interest to me.'

'But aren't they important if I'm to represent the Allegri Corporation at this—'

'Absolutely not.' I cut off the argument. 'And Joe Donnelly was wrong to give you that impression.' I was going to be having words with my friend to find out exactly what he'd said to Edie to give her the impression her background mattered—although I suspected Edie had simply got the wrong end of the stick; after all, Joe was as much of a mongrel as I was.

'What I'm interested in is your intellect and your ability to assess my guests' attitude to risk,' I reiterated. 'That's why I hired you and that's what I'm paying you for. And, believe me, I intend to get my money's worth. We'll meet each evening for a debrief with the rest of my management team after the guests have gone to bed—which will sometimes be at two or three in the morning. I'll expect you to be alert and informative and articulate about every aspect of your interactions—I'm a night owl and I tend to conduct most of my business at night. I'll also want a written analysis in the mornings before the next day's activities begin. And as much useful data as you can give me. I'll expect you to be my eyes and my ears at the tables whenever I'm not there. Believe me, your role here will not be easy. But pedigree means absolutely nothing to me. What I look for in an employee is results. And, more importantly, if you in any way think that someone is judging you I want you to tell me. As I have already explained…' I wished once again I hadn't blurted that information out, because she was looking at me now with a sort of hero-worship '…no one's as much of a mongrel as I am. And anyone who judges you for it would also judge me, so they're not someone I would want to do business with.'

'I won't disappoint you,' she said breathlessly. And I knew she wouldn't. I'd never seen someone so eager to please.

But the thought sent an unwelcome shaft of unease through me.

Her intellect, her data skills and her ability to read the play on the poker table weren't the only reasons I'd hired her. My gaze raked over the silky dress, which hugged her curves like a lover, and the heat in my groin became intense and insistent.

'But that's not the only reason I offered you this job,' I said, determined to be as open and honest with her as she had been with me—so that I could crush this foolish sense of connection once and for all. 'There's another reason I wanted you at my beck and call for the next ten days...'

I watched the pulse in her collarbone flutter.

'What's that?' she said, her voice coming out on a husky croak as her pupils darkened, and those expressive eyes became huge.

She had to know what I was referring to. She'd initiated that damn kiss. The kiss that had been firing my imagination and keeping me awake every night since. Perhaps she was being coy. I almost wished she was, but somehow I doubted it. There was something about her that seemed so fresh and young and forthright. And to think I'd once believed she was hard to read. At the moment she seemed far too easy to read.

'I think you know the reason,' I said.

Unable to quell the desire to touch her a moment longer, I lifted my hand and teased the lock of hair the stylist had left dangling. The temptation to feast on that damn mouth and finally ease the hunger in my groin was immense, but I resisted it.

I wanted her to come to me. No, I *needed* her to come to me. Then there would be no confusion—no blurring of the lines between her employment and her decision to spend time in my bed. So I dropped my hand.

Her breath gushed out, the pulse in her collarbone fluttering alarmingly as her breasts rose and fell in a staggered rhythm against the bodice of her dress.

'The chemistry between us is off the charts, *bella*,' I said, stating the obvious. 'I think we would be foolish not to enjoy it while we're here, in whatever down time we have.'

Her tongue darted out to lick her lips. My gaze fixed on her mouth. Damn, but I wanted to taste those lips again so badly.

'But anything that happens between us would be entirely your choice,' I continued, my voice now a husky croak. 'And would have absolutely no bearing on your employment with me. Is that understood?'

She nodded, her eyes still wide. The emotions that crossed her face—astonishment, confusion, arousal—would have been amusing if the erection now pounding in my pants wasn't getting all my attention. The important thing was that I could see no fear. And I'd take that.

The serving staff chose that moment to re-enter the room with our entrées. I directed her to sit down. 'I'm glad we got that settled. Now, do you want to join me for the next course and we can talk about what we're actually here to talk about?'

She nodded again, and regained her seat.

The remainder of the meal was predictably excruciating, for both of us. Every time she placed a morsel of food into that too kissable mouth, or leaned forward, allowing the candlelight to flicker over the hint of cleavage, my groin tightened, the pounding in my pants becoming unbearable. But I forced myself to focus on laying the groundwork for our professional relationship.

The only consolation was I could see her struggling to maintain her side of the conversation too. Somehow or other, we got through the meal without jumping each other.

I quickly discovered she was every bit as bright and intuitive as I had believed, and she, I hoped, discovered that I wouldn't pounce on her until she was ready.

But as I bid her goodnight I couldn't help bringing her trembling fingers to my lips. I kissed her knuckles, satisfied by the flare of heat she couldn't disguise.

'I'll be back in two days' time,' I said, a little disconcerted when I saw her shoulders slump with relief. Perhaps I hadn't been quite as unthreatening as I'd hoped. I would have to work on it. 'The guests arrive that afternoon so we can meet for lunch that day.'

'Okay, I'll work out the formulas we talked about,' she said breathlessly.

I had to give her points for remembering the discussion, which had slipped my mind already.

'Excellent, I look forward to it,' I said. 'Good night, *bella*,' I added, giving her permission to leave.

She nodded but, before she could hurry out of the room, I added, 'And remember, you are a free agent when it comes to anything other than work.'

'I know, Dante,' she said, the glow of pleasure in her eyes having a strange effect on me.

I realised it wasn't just my groin that was throbbing painfully as I watched her rush from the room. My heart felt as if it had expanded to twice its normal size and was thundering against my ribcage.

Dammit man, chill out.

I returned to my seat to nurse the last of my wine—to cool off and get this insatiable hunger into perspective. It occurred to me that it was probably a good thing I would be gone for the next two days, and once I returned there would be no time, for the first few days at least, for me to pursue Edie, because I would be far too busy—and so would she.

I hadn't lied, this week-long house party was important to my business—and I was not about to allow my desire for Edie Trouvé to get in the way of achieving everything I wanted to achieve. I'd been planning this event for months. I was on the verge of expanding the Allegri Corporation. I needed investors I could trust, and deciding who I did and did not want to invite into financial partnerships was crucial. I couldn't afford to get distracted from those goals.

But after those initial impressions had been made, and assuming Edie was as adept at what I was hiring her to do as she seemed, there would be time at the end of the week to indulge ourselves.

Assuming she chose to do so.

I stroked my thumb over the crystal, watched the red wine sparkle in the candlelight. The pounding in my groin increased as something raw clawed at me.

What would I do if she chose not to come to me?

I took a fortifying gulp of the expensive vintage, let the fruity flavours burst on my tongue—the moment of uncertainty reminding me unpleasantly of the boy I'd once been.

I swallowed and coughed out a rough laugh, realising how ludicrous the direction of my thoughts was.

The throaty sound—arrogant and assured—echoed off the antique furniture which had once belonged to a Portuguese prince. But which now belonged to me.

Don't be a damn fool, Dante. She wants you, just as much as you want her—you're not that feral kid any more.

This attraction was all about sex—and chemistry—I'd told her so myself.

I finished the wine.

All I had to do now was wait. And, luckily, I had something much more important to focus on than satisfying my libido—namely taking Allegri to the next level—to keep me busy in the meantime.

CHAPTER THIRTEEN

I BLINKED INTO the crisp morning light as it shone through the huge picture window in the guest villa's bedroom and checked the brand new, state-of-the-art smartphone I had been given a week ago by Joseph Donnelly as part of my employee package.

Pleasure rippled through me at the thought of another day working as part of Dante's elite management team. We'd been up till two o'clock last night, going through the individual reports by each member of the team. Dante had presided over the meeting in his office and even though it had been the middle of the night, the energy and enthusiasm in the room had been addictive.

I'd come to love those late-night meetings, when the guests had retired to their villas and we would gather—two other women and three men, all several years older than me—to pore over our individual reports and observations of everything that had gone on during the day and evening. Yesterday, Dante's events manager had arranged a flotilla of yachts and sailing boats to take the guests and the team to a picnic on a private island off the coast. There had been a lavish lunch arranged, not what I'd call a picnic, then water skiing and snorkelling safaris—and, for the less athletically inclined, sunbathing—in the afternoon, followed by an evening barbecue and then a night sail back to base for the evening rounds of poker and *vingt-et-un*. Dante had rather cleverly subbed all the guests a hundred thousand dollars' worth of chips for the week, with the promise that any profits they made by the end of the week would be theirs and any losses written off as a gesture of goodwill.

Last night's poker session had been my first chance to really shine. Everyone had been much more relaxed than the first night and, as a result, had bet more freely. I'd been able to gather much more data on their attitudes to risk. And when I'd detailed it all during our nightly round-up, in front of the other members of the team, and Dante, I'd felt Dante's encouragement—and his approval.

I was proving myself. Showing that his investment in me was worth it. I felt like a valued member of his team and it was intoxicating.

Pulling back the covers, I raced into the adjoining walk-in wardrobe and found the selection of swimsuits Nina had picked out for me. So far I'd only worn the one-piece ones, too shy to be seen by Dante wearing anything as skimpy as the bikinis she had selected.

My skin flushed.

Yesterday, Dante had asked me to join his crew for the evening sail back to La Villa Paradis and I'd imagined he'd had his eyes on me the whole time. Of course, he hadn't; that was just my overactive imagination. Since our dinner four days ago, he'd been nothing but professional with me. But it had still been a heady feeling—remembering the way he had looked at me that night at supper and the things he'd said.

I pulled the tiny triangles of blue Lycra out of the drawer and slipped them on. I'd never worn a bikini before which, considering I was half-French, was probably sacrilege.

I wasn't ashamed of my body; I'd inherited my mother's physique, slim but curvaceous. But I'd never worn anything so revealing before. Instead of feeling over-exposed though, awareness shimmered over my skin. And I imagined Dante looking at me, and liking what he saw, my breasts cupped by the stretchy fabric, my round hips and flat stomach displayed to their best advantage. I'd never felt so young and alive and carefree. And Dante was responsible for that, for freeing me and my sister from our debts and bringing me here and showing me he had faith in my abilities. I hadn't realised until these last few days of working with Dante and his team, and not having to worry about the basics—such as where the next meal was coming from—how much the last year, and even the years before that, had dragged me down with worry. I was only twenty-one years old, but I'd been burdened with so much grief and responsibility ever since our mother had died that I hadn't felt young in a long, long time.

I took a deep breath and flung the pashmina away which I had planned to wrap around my shoulders. I slipped on a pair of sandals and grabbed a towel from the pile in the bathroom.

There were three private beaches on the estate, with steps leading down to them from the extensive gardens. Two were large stretches of open sand well stocked with loungers, a beach bar where staff served a range of food and drink from 11:00 a.m. onwards, and hot showers so the guests could rinse off before returning to their accommodation. But two days ago I had found a tiny cove at the far end of the headland. The beach was a small crescent of white sand and there was an outdoor shower to rinse off and an unstaffed beach shelter furnished with lounging couches and a fridge stocked with delicacies. Despite those amenities, it was obviously too low-key for the guests because no one seemed to use it. I'd been there several times for a morning swim and had yet to meet anyone else there.

As a result, I had come to consider it my own private beach. I headed through the gardens for the entrance to the steps down to the cove, breathing in the fragrant scent of flowers, listening to the tinkle of the water fountains, admiring the view across the headland of the pastel-coloured houses of Villefranche on the other side of the bay.

My spirits were high, buzzing at the thought of taking an early morning swim in the cool blue ocean in my revealing bikini.

No one would see me but me. No one else would be up yet; our team didn't have to assemble for the morning briefing about today's activities—and the rundown of who to concentrate on and who Dante had already eliminated from his roster of possible investors—for another two hours. And none of the guests usually emerged until at least noon. But still, wearing the skimpy swimwear and going for a swim alone felt reckless, exciting, exhilarating.

I found the partially hidden entrance to the steps behind one of the garden follies—a Japanese pagoda with a pond full of koi carp. I rushed down the steps hewn into the rock-face, then stopped dead as I came to the platform above the cove.

Someone else was here, swimming across the inlet. His broad shoulders and dark head sliced through the waves in smooth, purposeful strokes.

Dante.

I recognised him instantly because of the way he moved, eating up the water, his powerful body forging its own path regardless of surf or tide.

I noticed the small pile of clothes on the sand. Was he swimming naked?

My breathing stopped at the errant thought, my heart thundering so hard against my ribs I became light-headed. I shrunk back against the warm rock-face, behind a lavender bush that grew out of the crevice, so that I could see him clearly but he could not see me.

I devoured the sight of him, those strong steady strokes echoing in my abdomen and making my breasts feel swollen and heavy, barely confined by my bikini.

At last he swam back towards the shore. And walked out of the surf, slicking his hair back. His body emerged from the sea and my breathing speeded up. The pounding in my chest plunged deep into my abdomen.

His torso was hard and contoured like a work of art; the water shining on his bronze skin shimmered in the sunlight and made him look like some sort of god. A sea king like Poseidon, powerful and indomitable. I was less than fifteen feet away from him but thankfully, because of the sound of the waves buffeting the shore, he couldn't hear my ragged breathing, which was becoming heavier by the second as I waited for him to emerge the rest of the way. From this distance I could see the white marks of scars that marred his skin and the dark ink of a tattoo that covered his left shoulder then looped around his neck. My heart hit my chest as I recalled his devastating revelations about his childhood four nights ago, and the guarded, wary way he had responded to my sympathy for that traumatised child. As if he had regretted revealing so much.

I swallowed down the thickening in my throat as I revisited the emotions that had bombarded me that night—horror for what that little boy must have endured, and huge admiration for the man he had become.

But then all coherent thought fled as Dante walked the rest of the way out of the water.

He *was* naked. And he looked utterly magnificent. I knew I should look away—I was spying on him—but I couldn't seem to detach my gaze from the masculine beauty of his nude body. The lean waist, the narrow hips, the muscular thighs and long legs, the bunch and flex of his abdominal muscles as he moved in sinuous motion. Adrenaline surged through me in a heady wave of arousal so fierce I felt giddy. My mouth dried to parchment as my gaze finally arrowed down through the magnificent V of his hip flexors to the nest of dark hair at his groin.

Mon Dieu.

He was very large. And long.

Weren't men supposed to shrink in the cold water?

Excitement and arousal warred with panic in the centre of my chest, but did nothing to counteract the deep throbbing in my sex at the sight of his naked penis.

My mind screamed at me to move, to flee, to scurry back up the beach steps before he caught me.

If I stayed, if he became aware of my presence, I knew that all bets would be off. I would be incapable of protecting myself from this rush of need. I would be forced to make the choice he had given me four days ago—and finally feed the hunger which had been building inside me for weeks, ever since our first and only kiss.

I tried to debate the pros and cons of taking that step, as he lifted a towel from the pile of clothing and dried himself in rough efficient strokes.

I still had a chance here. To escape this need, this longing.

But the insistent pulse in my sex refused to be silenced. And suddenly all I could think about was discovering what it would be like to become Dante's lover. Would I be totally overwhelmed again by the hunger that had thrilled me and frightened me ever since I had met him? Did I even care any more if I was?

This was not the man I had run from in Monaco. Back then he had been a distant, frightening figure. A man who could destroy me with a click of his fingers. But he had chosen not to do that; instead he'd given me a chance, a way out, when he didn't have to. He'd told me more than once that he wasn't a kind man, or a nice man, and on some levels I knew he wasn't kidding about that. He could be ruthless, he was ambitious and driven, because he'd had to be. He would be a difficult man to love, if not impossible. But this wasn't about love, I told myself staunchly as my heart all but choked me. This was about feeding the hunger, allowing myself to take something for myself. And I knew, whatever else happened, I trusted him. He would make this exciting, special, important—he'd promised me that much and I believed him.

No, he wasn't a nice man, or a kind man, but I sensed, beneath the scars and the tattoos, the rough upbringing and the dogged pursuit of power and status, and wealth, he was a good man.

And that was all I really needed him to be. He couldn't hurt me if I didn't let him.

When would I ever have a chance like this again? To take a man as hot and magnificent as Dante Allegri to be my lover? My first lover?

I was by nature a cautious person. I'd had to be. But as I stood there in the warming sunlight, my whole body alive with sensation and gripped by the deep visceral tug of longing, I knew I didn't want to be cautious any longer. Not about this. Because of my upbringing, because of spending so much of my childhood watching my mother falling in and out of love with powerful men, I was sure I could keep my heart safe while my body reached out to this man. And took everything it wanted. Everything he had promised me.

He had tugged on his shorts and was busy running the towel over his hair as I stepped out of my hiding place.

As if he sensed me, his head rose suddenly and his movements stilled.

I could feel his gaze burning over every inch of my exposed skin—and there was a lot of it—as I walked down the last of the steps to the beach on shaky legs.

He didn't stop looking at me, his gaze roaming over me as his hand fell to his side and the towel dropped to the sand.

The adrenaline rioting through my system gave me the strength to walk the rest of the way across the warm sand towards him. I knew somehow that he wouldn't take a single step towards me. It was all part of the promise he'd made me. That this was my choice.

But, as I approached him, I could see the arousal burning in his eyes, inching out the blue of his irises and turning them to black as his pupils dilated. His breathing was as heavy as my own and that matching need somehow calmed the last of the nerves knotting in my belly.

'Bella...' The endearment which I had come to adore issued from those sensual lips on a husky croak of need as I finally reached him. 'What the hell are you doing here?'

Satisfaction surged through me at the dark frown, the confusion matched by the hunger in his gaze.

I might be woefully inexperienced sexually, but I felt bold, brazen even, in my excuse for a bikini. He'd given me the choice and I was making it. No regrets, no excuses, no turning back.

'Spying on you,' I said on a tortured huff of breath. Unafraid. And unashamed.

I let my gaze drift over him in return, and let every ounce of my excitement show as the muscles of his six-pack rippled with tension, and the thick ridge stretching his boxer briefs lengthened.

The erection looked enormous, but I didn't care. I wasn't

scared. I knew it would hurt but my sex had melted, the liquid tug between my thighs throbbing painfully now with the desire to feel that thick ridge thrusting inside me.

A cold knuckle tucked under my chin and he lifted my face to his.

'You're playing with fire, Edie. Unless you want me to make love to you in the next five seconds, you need to leave now.'

Make love to you.

They were only words, I knew that, to describe a basic, elemental desire. But they pierced my heart as I forced a smile to my lips, trying to appear assured and uninhibited.

I knew instinctively that I needed to keep exactly how inexperienced I was hidden from him. Or this affair would be over before it had begun.

Dante wasn't looking for intimacy—his horrified reaction to my sympathy four nights ago had told me that much. And neither was I, despite the heavy thuds of my heartbeat. I might be a virgin, but I had always known the vast difference between lust and love—unlike my mother… Perhaps because of my mother and all the heartache I'd watched her suffer over men who had wanted her body but never her heart. Her mistake had been to think that by giving one she would get the other. I though, was a realist who would never make that mistake.

'I'm not going anywhere,' I said.

I saw his control snap, and the surge of adrenaline flowed through my veins as he swore softly and then grasped my upper arms to yank me into his embrace.

He cupped my bottom, pressing the hard ridge of his erection into my belly. I reached up and sunk my fingers into the wet silk of his hair as his lips sucked on my collarbone, finding the place where my pulse pounded and throbbed.

His chilly fingers sunk beneath the scrap of blue Lycra and I bucked against him, shocked by the intimacy of his touch as the heel of his hand pressed against my vulva and then he found the hot nub of my clitoris.

'*Bella*, you're so wet for me already,' he murmured against my neck, stroking, circling, caressing and making my whole body dance to his tune.

He dragged off the bikini top, snapping the strap, and covered my swollen breast with his mouth, while continuing to play with his thumb, devious strokes that thrust me into a maelstrom of needs.

Part of me panicked at the speed and intensity of the feelings engulfing me, but as the waves rose up to batter my body, the arrow of sensation in my breast as he suckled hard at the nipple reverberated in my sex. The sobs of my fulfilment echoed off the surrounding rocks, drowning out the sound of the sea, the surf and the thundering beating of my heart.

'Come for me now,' he demanded.

I hung suspended for what felt like for ever but could only have been a few seconds, then flew over, my fingers tugging at his hair, my body bucking furiously as I ground my sex against his hand, his thumb having located the perfect spot to force me over that high wide ledge.

I crashed down, my besieged body shuddering from an orgasm so sudden and intense I felt as if I'd survived a war.

I had barely come back to my senses when I felt the sand shift beneath my feet.

He had scooped me into his arms, I realised. My eyelids fluttered open and my gaze fixed on his chin, and the small crescent-shaped scar that cut through the morning stubble on his top lip.

'Thank you,' I muttered.

'You're welcome.' He gave a throaty chuckle. 'We're

not finished yet though,' he said as he carried me into the beach shelter and placed me gently on one of the long cushioned couches.

He touched his thumb to my reddened nipple, played with the pebbled peak. I felt the flush of colour spread up to my hairline, knowing what a spectacle I made, lying there, all languid and sated, the bikini bra hanging off my shoulder.

He grinned, then plucked the strings that still held the garment on and drew it away. As I laid on my back topless, I shivered, seeing the feral light in his eyes. His grin died as he made quick work of the two bows that tied on the bikini bottom and tugged that off too.

Leaning over me, he swirled his tongue around my already tender nipples. I gasped, shaken by the swift return of arousal. I had thought I was sated. I was wrong.

I could hear the rush of the ocean in my ears, feel the warm breeze flowing over my over-sensitised skin, every part of me becoming an erogenous zone—throbbing with life and passion as he kissed and nipped, licked and caressed every inch of my skin.

I was writhing, the desire so intense it was almost pain when he finally parted the slick folds of my sex and lapped at the very heart of me. How could I be wild for him again so soon?

I moaned, about to go over again from the tantalising caresses, the wet suction of his lips on that swollen nub, when he rose over me. His broad shoulders cut out the sun as he stood up.

'Hold that thought, *bella*,' he said, his voice so low I could barely make out the words over the persistent thud of my pulse in my ears.

He shucked his shorts and the giant erection sprang free. Long and thick, it bowed up towards his belly button. I had a momentary fear that something so large and hard would never fit inside me, but I couldn't take my eyes away.

'I don't have protection with me,' he said as he grasped the base of the erection and stroked it absently. 'But I want so badly to feel you come apart around me,' he added, becoming even bigger and harder as I watched. 'I promise I am clean, and I will pull out in time.'

A shiny drop of moisture appeared at the tip. I was so fascinated and so turned-on I could hardly talk, let alone think. The juices between my thighs flowed freely, the desire to feel that thick length inside me unbearable. I licked my lips, fixated on the sight of him, and gloried in the thought that I had done that to him.

'*Bella*, look at me,' he ordered and my head jerked up to meet his gaze. He looked amused. 'Is that okay?'

It took me a moment to register what he was asking. The blush intensified as I realised he'd caught me gawping at his erection like a child in a sweet factory.

'Yes, I'm clean,' I said. 'And I'm on the Pill,' I said, for once impossibly grateful that I had started taking the medication to regulate my periods—which had become erratic, my doctor had insisted, because of stress. But I didn't feel stressed now; I felt languid and exhilarated all at the same time. 'And I want you inside me too,' I said, just in case there was any doubt in his mind.

'Grazie Dio,' he murmured, the muffled curse full of the strain it was taking him to go slowly, hold back until he had my consent.

Somehow the thought of that had my heart beating double time in my chest as I watched him climb onto the lounger. His body looked so wonderful, the many imperfections as beautiful as the sleek muscles, the deeply tanned skin, the sprinkle of hair that brushed against my trembling legs and my reddened nipples. He kissed me, his tongue tangling with mine as he lifted my leg and hooked it over his. I tasted sea salt and the musty scent of my own arousal as the kiss deepened and became hungrier. The huge head of his erection nudged at the swollen folds he had primed so perfectly.

Then he thrust hard and deep. The pinching pain shocked me, the stretched feeling becoming unbearable as he plunged through the barrier of my virginity.

I bit down on my lip, swallowing the whimper of distress, as my tender flesh adjusted to the immense weight inside me. I felt impaled, conquered, overpowered.

He stilled and stared down at me. I saw shock, then confusion, then suspicion cross his face, before he masked it. For several torturous seconds I lay there shivering, waiting for him to pull out. I thought he had figured out that I was a virgin and he was angry. But as the blush fired back across my cheeks, that assured smile returned to his lips and all he said was, 'You're incredibly tight, *bella*. Am I hurting you?'

I shook my head, the muscles of my sex relaxing at last. He was still too big, too overwhelming, the intrusion still sore, still too much, but I didn't want him to stop. And I definitely didn't want him to figure out my secret—that I had no experience of sex at all. That I was a fraud.

'I can make it better—just relax,' he said, still lodged so deep inside me I was sure I could feel him in my throat. He placed a tender kiss on my lips. Then focused all his attention on my nipple again, licking and sucking the responsive flesh. He stayed inside me without moving, allowing me to adjust to his size, his girth. The darts of pleasure began to build again, and the muscles of my sex released him a little more.

At last he found the tender nub of my clitoris with that clever thumb again, and began to circle it. My sex softened, allowing him to move, rocking out, pressing back in slow, careful thrusts.

'How does that feel?' he said as he pressed deeper, but there was no pain now, only the exquisite waves of pleasure, building, breaking.

'Good,' I managed around the thickness in my throat, at the care he'd taken with me.

He pulled me under him completely and gripped my thighs, positioning me, and angling my hips, until I was wide open to him. The slow, sure, steady strokes, became harder, faster, deeper. His fingers dug into my buttocks as he forced me to take the full measure of him, butting a place that had the waves building with staggering speed.

My hands grasped his sweat-slicked shoulders, trying to cling onto my sanity as the titanic climax raced towards me.

It hit me hard, crashing into me with the force and fury of a tsunami. I cried out, swept away by the conflagration of sensation charging through my body. He grunted as I massaged his thick length, then reared back, the hoarse shout echoing off the cliffs above us as his hot seed spurted against my belly and he collapsed on top of me.

I held onto him, the shelf of his tattooed shoulder pressed me into the cushions as his jagged breathing matched my own. The haze of afterglow covered me like a golden cloak full of sparkling lights, twinkling around me and sprinkling fairy dust over my skin. I tried to suppress the fanciful thought, but the intensity of my orgasm was working against me. Everywhere we touched I could feel him, imprinted on my flesh for ever.

As I stared at the blue sky above me, the sunlight warmed my skin and my heart expanded against my ribs as his hard length finally began to soften against my belly. But as much as I tried to dismiss the overly romantic images still flickering through my brain, and that compelling feeling of contentment and security—and concentrate on the small aches and pains brought about by the primitive fury of our lovemaking—I couldn't seem to qualify it, or even acknowledge the truth, that everything I was thinking and feeling in this moment was simply the intense physical aftermath of my first multiple orgasm.

Any more than I could ignore the clenching sensation in my chest and the desire to lie there for ever—safe and secure in his arms.

CHAPTER FOURTEEN

SHE WAS A VIRGIN, you idiot. She tricked you. And now she'll expect more from you than you can ever give. Or would want to give, I added swiftly, as my mind tried to engage with what had just happened.

The recriminations swirled around in my brain, but the ripples of afterglow still pulsing through my body made it hard for me to regret what I had done.

Her belly twitched against my softening erection and I felt the tingle of arousal at the base of my spine as I began to harden again.

What the...? This was madness. How could I possibly want her again so soon?

The realisation shocked me, enough to have me lifting up and rolling away from her. I lay on my back beside her and covered my eyes with my forearm.

I had felt her flinch as I drew out, but she said nothing as we lay there together, getting our breath back. Shame hung over me, not just because I had taken her with so little finesse, ploughing into her tight flesh like a battering ram, but at the knowledge that I could want to ravage her again so soon when she must be sore as hell.

I struggled to control my desire and willed my breathing to even out. She lay next to me on the lounger. I should move. I should offer to wash off my seed and the blood that had to be there. Thank God I had pulled out before I ejaculated, despite her assurances she was on the Pill. Surely that could have been a lie too, just like the pretence of sexual experience.

Dammit, why had she given herself to me so easily, so freely? Hadn't I told her exactly how much I was prepared to offer? I felt like a bastard now and I didn't like it. But what I liked even less was the urge to take her sweet, succulent and now no doubt bruised body back into my arms and apologise for what I'd done.

It wasn't my fault she'd remained silent. I'd given her ample chances to stop me, but she hadn't. Why hadn't she? What exactly was she expecting to happen now?

But instead of the emotional manipulations I expected to hear, instead of the muffled tears maybe because I had deflowered her with so little care or attention, I felt her fingers touch my arm. Tentative and halting.

I lifted my forearm to find her leaning over me, her face a picture of flushed arousal. Still. What was up with that? She couldn't possibly still desire me.

'Is everything okay, Dante?' she asked and I could hear the concern in her voice.

I huffed out a laugh that sounded strained and forced, but I could see her concern for me was genuine.

What on earth was going on? She was looking at me as if I were the injured party, instead of the other way around.

'Everything's terrific,' I said, still waiting for the other shoe to drop, or rather the axe to fall on my head, but instead of railing at me or demanding to know what my intentions were now, the sweet, unbearably sexy smile that I had only seen once before curved her lips.

I tried to quash the answering smile that wanted to curve my lips in response but there was no help for it. She wasn't going to mention her virginity, or the ruthless way I had plunged into her or the fact that I hadn't stopped when I should have done, or apologised even, like the heartless bastard I was. She wasn't even going to mention my loss of control and the fact I had carried on making love to her.

Could she actually be that guileless? That sweet? That innocent? Because it seemed that she was, and I couldn't seem to decide what I felt about that.

On the one hand it was going to let me off this hook very nicely indeed—because if she wasn't about to draw attention to her virginity, I certainly was not... But it also made her seem even more vulnerable than she had before—when I'd walked in on her being beaten by Carsoni's goon. But now the man hurting her and treating her without the proper care was me.

'You enjoyed it?' she said, but I could hear the question.

I rolled back towards her and stroked the side of her face with my thumb; the grinding feeling of inadequacy and shame and futile temper I hadn't wanted to acknowledge released in my chest.

'*Bella*, couldn't you tell?' I said.

The blush, which I had found so fascinating when I'd first met her, lit up her cheeks again. But now I knew exactly where that blush originated, from an openness and honesty far greater than I had already realised, it didn't just fascinate me, it captivated me. And although I knew I shouldn't, I had the strangest feeling of satisfaction that, for whatever reason, she had chosen me to be her first.

Maybe it wasn't that significant for her, that was why she hadn't mentioned it. And why she clearly didn't want me to mention it either—which was fine by me. But that didn't stop me from knowing. And wondering why on earth she would have chosen me. I hoped to hell it wasn't some foolish notion that I would give her more but it seemed so far as if my deeply cynical reaction to her virginity had been an overreaction, to say the least.

With that in mind, I needed to be casual now. Not to make a big deal of any of this. I forced myself to relax and smile back at her, even though the tightening in my chest felt far too significant.

'I… Yes, of course I could tell,' she said, feigning an experience I knew she didn't have. Why her little pretence should suddenly seem appealing instead of threatening or suspicious I had no idea but I decided to go with it.

'I should…' She thrust her thumb over her shoulder, pointing towards the shower at the bottom of the cliff steps. 'I should go and shower…' She smiled. 'I have an important meeting with my boss in an hour and a half.'

She grabbed a towel from the pile by the lounger and wrapped it around that luscious body. I grabbed one too, to cover myself, because I could feel myself getting hard again and I didn't want to scare her off.

Although she didn't seem scared. Which I decided was good. Once wasn't going to be enough for either one of us, but we needed to establish some parameters for this… hook-up. Because that's all this could ever be. She seemed to already realise that, which was also good, I supposed. And while I knew her attempts to appear blasé and urbane about what we'd done were really just an act, I didn't have a problem with that either. But not to the point that I was going to allow her to rush off now—or pretend that nothing had happened when I saw her again at the team briefing at eleven.

I had never slept with an employee before and certainly not one of my engagement team. But I didn't see why it should be a problem. We were all adults. Consenting adults. And everyone knew I didn't play favourites in a business situation. Every single person on my team had earned their place there. And Edie more than most. Her work so far had been exemplary. She was observant, erudite and incredibly sharp and that was before you even factored in her exceptional analytical abilities and her creative use of data to rationalise and assess the investment potential of each of the candidates we were considering. Not only had she worked hard over the last week and a half, she had impressed every member of the team and earned her place. And I knew how much that meant to her, after our conversation over dinner four nights ago. After the abuse she had clearly suffered because of her mother's behaviour, Edie had wrongly believed she had a lot to prove.

Considering that abuse, I would hazard a guess that was why she didn't want anyone knowing that we were an item. Because the professionalism she had done so much to achieve might be compromised.

Unfortunately though, keeping our liaison a secret wasn't going to work for me.

So when she went to leave, I grasped her wrist. 'Not so fast, Edie.'

She sat down on the lounger, her hands twisting on the towel she had wrapped around that delectable body.

'At the meeting today, and during the rest of this week,' I said, 'the guests and the team are going to know we have been intimate.'

She blinked, the blush exploding on her cheeks again. 'How?'

I had to resist the urge to laugh at the gaucheness of the question. Did she have any idea how she looked right now—like a woman who had been well and truly…? I cut off the crude word before I could even think it. She wasn't a whore, like my mother had been, like her own mother had been. In fact she was exactly the opposite. She didn't deserve to be thought of in that way. But that didn't mean

I was going to avoid stating the obvious. If she wanted to pretend she was experienced, I was entitled to treat her as if she were.

'Because I plan to sleep with you again. And I'm not about to keep it a secret. In fact,' I added, thinking of the practicalities, because from the look of stunned disbelief on her face she was clearly incapable of doing so. 'I would like to have your belongings moved into my suite of rooms. It seems pointless us staying at opposite ends of the estate. Logistically speaking. There's going to be little enough downtime given the roster of events Evan has planned for the remainder of the week. If we're going to make the most of the time we have available it makes sense for us to stay in the same place. And my suite is a great deal bigger than yours.'

'But...' she actually sputtered, her blush now radioactive, which I found ridiculously charming. It shouldn't matter to me, but it felt oddly exhilarating knowing I was the first man, the only man, she had ever been in a relationship with. 'Won't that compromise my position with the team?' she said, confirming my suspicions about her insecurities.

'Absolutely not. What you do in your spare time... What we both do in our spare time, for that matter... With each other. Is no one else's business. Believe me, you have more than proved yourself with every member of the team, including me, and no one is going to question that.' A flush of pleasure lit her eyes at the praise and the strange clenching in my chest increased. I forced it down. It wasn't as if I was complimenting her for any other reason than she had earned it. 'Plus, I've seen how some of the male guests have been sniffing around you,' I added, because now we had slept together it didn't seem inappropriate to admit to the jealousy that had gripped me every time one of the bastards even glanced at her. ‘I don’t like it. As long as they know you’re now with me, they’ll back off, which will save me the trouble of having to punch anyone. Which could get awkward, let’s face it, if they turn out to be one of the people we choose as an investor,’ I finished, only half joking.

‘You would punch one of the guests?’ She sounded both horrified and astonished. But the flush of colour told a slightly different story—which I suspected she was wholly unaware of—that having a man prepared to fight for her was a novel, but not entirely unwelcome, experience. I thought of the father who had refused to acknowledge her and couldn’t help the sudden desire to punch him too.

‘If a man got too familiar with you, yes, I’d punch him in a minute,’ I confirmed as I tucked a tendril of hair behind her ear. I let my thumb glide down the side of her neck, to caress the pulse which hammered her collarbone. I could see the beginnings of beard burn where I had devoured the soft flesh earlier. I would have to be more careful with her, I noted; her skin was so delicate. ‘I don’t share,’ I added, which was true. I insisted all relationships I had were mutually exclusive, no matter how short. But the strange surge of possessiveness at the thought of any other man touching her, or even looking at her, was something entirely new.

I dismissed the thought. It was only because she was so young and so inexperienced, and she was also in my employ, that I felt protective towards her. It would fade, along with my hunger for her. But, until it did, I didn’t see a problem with indulging myself. And her.

‘So how do you feel about having your belongings moved into my suite?’ I asked.

She hesitated, tugging that lush bottom lip with her teeth as she considered my request, and for a split second my pulse rate sped up—at the insane thought that she might refuse me. Of course she would not; she had enjoyed the sex as much as I had after that initial discomfort, I was sure about that now. And anyway, if she refused I was more than capable of persuading her. But weirdly, despite all my qualifications, my pulse remained elevated and erratic until she stopped biting her lip and nodded.

'Okay,' she said, the eager smile and the flicker of excitement in her eyes captivating me as much as that damn blush. 'If you insist,' she said.

'I do,' I murmured, unable to prevent an equally eager smile—at the thought of all the pleasure we would have after hours. I gave her a friendly pat on the butt. 'Now, you'd better go shower,' I said. 'Or you'll be late for work, and I know what a hard taskmaster your boss is.'

She laughed, the sound so light and sweet and carefree, my pulse rate spiked again, for an entirely different reason. But as she stood, with the towel still wrapped tightly around her lush curves, she looked down at me, her smile turning sultry and sexy and remarkably bold for a young woman who had only just been initiated into the joys of sex. An odd sense of pride gripped me at yet more evidence that my Edie was an exceptionally fast learner.

'Are you sure you don't want to join me?' she said, flicking her gaze provocatively towards the open shower used to rinse off the sea salt.

Blood surged into my groin at the image of her wet and dripping, those lush curves covered in soap suds as my hands teased her nipples and explored her warm flesh.

Whoa, ragazzo.

I shifted on the lounger, but kept the towel pressed firmly over my growing erection to hide my reaction to her bold suggestion.

As much as I would love to take her up on her offer, I knew she had to be sore and I didn't want to risk hurting her by taking things too far. Too soon.

While her flesh might be willing, mine was far too weak. Or, rather, not nearly weak enough.

'I think I will stay here and enjoy the view instead,' I said, with as casual a tone as I could muster, knowing it was going to be torture. 'You have exhausted me, *bella*,' I lied, but I was glad I had when she laughed with obvious pleasure, like the fledging man-eater she was. 'And we don't want to both be late for work.'

She nodded, again revealing that artless smile.

I watched her walk to the shower, unable to detach my gaze as she dropped the towel and put on a display worthy of a seasoned courtesan as she washed her beautiful body—a display which was all the more arousing for being entirely unconscious.

I waved to her as she left the beach, having slipped into one of the towelling robes left for the guests. I finally managed to drag my gaze off her as she disappeared up the beach steps. I would need to get my reaction to her under ruthless control before our morning team briefing, I realised, or all the promises I'd made to maintain our professional relationship in the professional spaces we shared would be shot to hell.

I gathered the triangles of blue fabric I had ripped off her earlier, intending to dispose of them for her and order her another bikini—because I was already anticipating the sight of those lush curves so temptingly confined again. But as I climbed off the lounger I noticed the spots of blood she had also left behind. Along with her innocence.

Not that I had needed any confirmation of her virginity after our encounter, but the sight had my heartbeat stuttering. And, although I knew it was a little disingenuous, I couldn't help making a silent vow as I stared at the evidence of her trust in me.

No woman had ever given me such a gift. And, while

I hadn't asked for it, and did not intend to acknowledge it, I felt a strange sense of responsibility towards her because of it.

This liaison wouldn't last. I would soon grow bored and restless, as I always did, and she would eventually discover I was a dangerous man to become too attached to. Luckily Edie was a smart, intuitive woman, however inexperienced, and she would soon figure out the truth about me, if she hadn't already.

But as I stood under the shower myself and took my erection in hand to give myself some necessary relief, I made Edie one promise. Whatever happened, I would endeavour to make this liaison as fun and pleasurable for her as it was for me.

Given my appetite for her—and the intensity of our sexual chemistry—I was liable to make a lot of demands in the next days as we enjoyed each other. But I would be careful to gauge her reaction and make sure that I never asked too much. I would take nothing for granted and I would also attempt to smooth out at least a few of my rough edges. And, most importantly of all, I would let her down gently when this liaison reached its inevitable conclusion. Because, however bold and brave and intelligent Edie was, she was still entirely new to this—and she certainly hadn't picked the most tender, or refined, or gentle of men to initiate her.

And, if nothing else, I didn't want her to ever regret that.

CHAPTER FIFTEEN

I STOOD ON the balcony of Dante's suite, watching the guests mingle below me in the torchlit gardens in their designer ball gowns and tuxedos—like exotic peacocks displaying their wealth and status in the summer night. *Cordon bleu* canapés and vintage champagne were being served on sterling silver platters, and I could hear the strains of the orchestra in the ballroom below me playing the opening bars of a Viennese waltz for those people elegant enough, or merry enough, to brave the dance floor.

The night was perfect, and a little surreal, and I was a part of it. An essential part of it.

Nerves and excitement tangled in the pit of my stomach, going some way to alleviate the bubble of regret that had been lodged in my throat all day.

I'd had such an amazing time in the last five days, ever since Dante and I had started sleeping together. The sex had been… Well, nothing short of a revelation. I'd never felt more alive or present, more hungry and yet sated all at the same time. Dante had kept to his word, and been absolutely incredible—making me feel both cherished and desired, while also keeping a clear separation between my work responsibilities and the things we did after hours. Despite agreeing to allow our affair to become public knowledge, I had been unbearably nervous that first day. Surely the other team members would resent my involvement with Dante, would judge me for it. And in some ways I'd been prepared for it, had even understood it.

But no such problems had arisen. If anything, most of the team had found it amusing and kind of sweet. Collette had even whispered to me that first day, while she was supervising having my belongings moved to Dante's quarters, 'You are good for him. He has been much less of a taskmaster this week than usual.'

I knew she was joking. Dante wasn't a taskmaster at all; he was focused, yes, and he had high expectations which he expected to be met by every one of his employees. But he was also fair and very good at communicating those expectations, so there was no confusion.

But still, I had basked in Collette's approval and laughed with Jenny Caldwell, the middle-aged woman who ran his accounts department, when she had winked at me after Dante had grabbed my hand and dragged me out of the office when last night's final briefing had finished.

Of course, the attitude of the staff had had a lot to do with how Dante had handled the whole situation. Not only had he been forthright and pragmatic about our 'arrangement', but he'd also made a point of showing me no favouritism within the team. He'd been equally frank with the guests—making a point of treating me with respect in front of them, but also making no bones about claiming me as his during the leisure time we had together, when he never missed an opportunity to touch me or caress me.

And he simply hadn't given me a chance to be ashamed of how much I enjoyed his attentiveness.

There had only been one small moment of unpleasantness, with a woman called Elise Durand, the CEO of a large French hospitality firm, who had approached me yesterday. In the few interactions I had had with the woman at the poker table, my assessment of her business acumen and her approach to risk had been favourable and I knew she was one of the front runners for investor status. It was quite possible Dante and his two top financiers were offering her a stake in the new expansion right now. A chill ran up my spine as I recalled what she had said to me the night before, as I was rushing through the gardens, already anticipating the rendezvous at our private cove which I had arranged with Dante for a late-night swim.

'You remind me a great deal of your mother, Edie. She also had a taste for powerful men and knew how to use it to her best advantage.'

I watched the moon glow over the bay, the lights of Villefranche in the distance twinkling, and forced myself to ignore the feeling of inadequacy that had assailed me. How stupid, to let something so innocuous ruin my happy buzz. It had been a throwaway comment, which I had taken far too much to heart, because I was over-sensitive about my mother's reputation.

I hadn't mentioned the comment to Dante. Or anyone else. Because I didn't want to appear unprofessional, and I certainly didn't want to prejudice Dante's decision about whom he invited to invest in his company because of our fling and my own insecurities.

The bubble of regret expanded another inch.

The fling that was going to end tonight.

I swallowed, trying not to let the feeling of ennui—of sadness—get the better of me. I'd always known this would be a few days of bliss. Dante hadn't promised more than a quick fling and I hadn't asked him for more. Which was for the best, I now realised. Because, even after only five days as his lover, I knew I was sinking too deep into this relationship. Wanting things from it that I knew I could never have.

Already, I was consumed with anticipation every time I saw him. I reacted with complete abandon to even the slightest show of affection or attention from him. And I had become utterly addicted to his lovemaking.

A blush warmed my cheeks despite the sea breeze, as I recalled the shameless way I had responded the night before. To be fair, that wasn't entirely my fault, I added to myself. Dante, I had discovered, could be an absolute devil.

Last night, on the beach, almost as if he had sensed my loss of confidence after my encounter with Elise, he had worked me into a frenzy of need and longing, until all I could focus on, and all I could think about, was him.

Using his tongue and his teeth in ways he already knew would drive me wild, he had given me mini-orgasm after mini-orgasm without ever giving me enough relief to completely satisfy me. Eventually I had been a quivering bundle of raw nerves and desperate needs. I had cried myself hoarse, literally begging him to thrust deep enough and hard enough to release me from the sensual torture—and, when he finally had, the orgasm had been so powerful I was pretty sure I had actually passed out.

But it was the way he had washed me so tenderly afterwards, and insisted on carrying me back through the gardens and all the way into our suite of rooms, that had all but destroyed me.

I'd fallen into a deep sleep—the dreams of belonging, of safety and security all the more devastating when I had woken this morning with his strong body wrapped around me and he'd made love to me again with a ruthless tenderness which I had convinced myself for one bright shining moment meant much more than it did.

I heard the outer door to our suite open and Dante's footsteps on the carpeting.

My heart leapt into my throat on cue as I turned and

watched him walk towards me. He looked dashing and debonair in the tailored tuxedo, reminding me of the man I'd met that first night who had terrified me on some visceral level.

He terrified me even more now, I realised, because I couldn't seem to control the erratic beat of my heart as he gathered me into his arms.

'At last, the work is finally finished, the investors are in place and we can celebrate,' he murmured, nuzzling my neck, raising goosebumps that rioted over my collarbone and arrowed into my sex—which had already begun to melt at the sight of him, readying itself for the erection that pressed insistently against my belly.

'That's wonderful,' I said, trying to smile, and swallow down the bubble that only got larger at the thought that we only had tonight now, before this affair would be over.

He drew back and held out my arms, his gaze becoming dark and intense as it roamed over the satin ball gown Nina had had made for me especially for tonight's occasion. 'You look absolutely stunning,' he said.

The familiar blush flared across my cleavage. He never forgot to compliment me, to make his appreciation and his approval known. And I realised I had become completely addicted to that too. My skin burned at the reminder that Nina had insisted I wear nothing under the gown.

'So do you,' I said, letting my gaze roam over him in turn. He really did look magnificent in the dark evening wear. I imagined the scars that lurked beneath it, which I had explored with my fingers and lips countless times now. They were a testament, just as the suit was, to how hard he'd worked to escape the degradation of his upbringing. A stupid spurt of pride at his achievements worked its way up my torso, even though I'd had nothing whatsoever to do with them.

'Hey?' He lifted my chin and met my gaze. 'Is something wrong?'

'No, nothing,' I lied easily enough. I didn't want to mar our last night together with my ridiculous emotions. 'I just wish we could stay and celebrate here,' I said boldly, which wasn't a lie.

He let out a hoarse chuckle. 'You and me both.'

He gripped my fingers and gave them a squeeze. 'But I'm afraid we're going to have to make an appearance. I wouldn't want that beautiful gown to go to waste...' His pupils darkened as he led me towards the door, his thumb rubbing my palm possessively. 'Before I rip it off you,' he added, sending the familiar shiver of anticipation through me.

I let out a strained laugh as we walked down the wide sweeping staircase towards the ballroom. People turned to stare, and I had the weirdest sensation of being like a princess at a ball—young and desperately in lust with the handsome prince every other woman here wanted but couldn't have, because he had chosen me.

The sensation of acceptance, of belonging, was fanciful and fleeting for sure, but still I rejoiced in the renewed leap in my heartbeat.

Why not enjoy tonight, and worry about the struggle to keep my emotions in check tomorrow, when I returned to Belle Rivière—and reality intruded again?

'Who did you decide to offer investor status to in the end?' I asked, as Dante took a glass of champagne off the tray of a passing waiter and handed it to me.

'Devon O'Reilly and the consortium from Le Grange,' Dante said, mentioning an Irish racehorse owner and a group of hedge fund managers, both of whom I'd recommended. There was only one other person I'd recommended.

'Not Elise Durand?' I asked, surprised but also stupidly pleased. I tried to quell the trickle of pleasure that she hadn't been invited to invest after all, because it made me feel petty and insecure.

'No, not Elise,' he said, his brows lowering as he watched me over his glass. 'Although it might have been nice if I had found out about her unsuitability from you, instead of Collette.'

'I… I don't understand.'

I lowered my glass from my lips, scared to take another sip in case I choked on the emotion currently rising up my torso.

Had he found out about Elise's comment to me from Collette? And if he had, why was he so angry about it, because I could see the temper swirling in his eyes?

'She insulted you, Edie,' he said, giving me the answer to a question I had been too scared to ask. 'Do you really think I would want to do business with her after that? I had her escorted off the estate as soon as I found out. And I intend to make it known that I refused to do business with her or her company.'

'I'm not sure she meant it as an insult,' I said, not sure why I was defending her. Because it seemed very obvious to me now that's exactly what she had intended—to undermine and belittle me. And of course she had succeeded, tapping into my insecurities, my feelings of inadequacy with a simple offhand remark. But what seemed so much more dangerous now was Dante's reaction. Because he hadn't just spotted the insult before me, he had jumped to my defence. And was clearly furious on my behalf. Enough to base an important business decision on it. It suddenly felt like too much. Not just his decision to defend me and protect me, and do something as extreme as having Elise Durand kicked off the estate, but also my reaction to that response.

I had tried so hard not to fall in love with this man. And I'd succeeded, despite the violent intensity of his lovemaking, despite the respect he showed me at every turn, despite the way he had cherished and complimented me. But I could feel myself slipping—no, crashing—over the edge as he stared back at me now with outrage and annoyance, at me as much as Elise, etched on his face.

His emotions were rarely so unguarded, and that unsettled me too. That he would let me see how much Elise's insult had angered him.

'Don't ever apologise for or excuse other people's prejudices again,' he said, or rather commanded, and just like that I felt my heart drop like a stone. Wow, I really was a hopeless case, I realised vaguely, as I tumbled into the abyss—unsure of where I would land but unable to break my fall.

How could I be falling in love with this man, not because of his sensitive nurturing qualities, not because of his protectiveness, or even his epic skills in the sack, but because of his quick-fire temper, his possessiveness and his overbearing arrogance? It would be utterly tragic... If it weren't so... I took a shuddering breath, trying to collect myself and fight back the tears threatening to spill over my lids... If it weren't so wonderful.

'You're not your mother,' he continued, still lecturing me and clearly completely oblivious to the emotions I was struggling to get a grip on. 'And no one gets to judge you or insult you because of the mistakes she made. You're worth so much more than that. Do you understand?'

I nodded, because my heart was too swollen and rammed too far up my throat to attempt coherent speech.

He paused, finally realising that he was browbeating me. 'All right, then. Let's forget about it now,' he said, sounding disconcerted for the first time since I'd met him. Was he as stunned by his impassioned defence of me as I was?

I thought of his own background, the horrors of his childhood which he had outlined to me in such stark, unemotional terms. As if they'd happened to another man, as if he'd come to terms with them years ago and got over them. And now I wondered—was that really the case? Perhaps he believed he had been unaffected, that he had risen above those traumas and moved on. But surely he hadn't, if he could hear about the fairly minor slight Elise had subjected me to—which, I would hazard a guess, was nothing like the kind of insults he had probably suffered—and be so enraged on my behalf.

'She's gone and she's not coming back,' he added.

He tossed the last of the champagne back, and I wondered if his mouth was now as dry as mine.

'Do you want the rest of that?' he asked, nodding at my full glass as he dumped his own empty glass on a waiter's tray.

I shook my head, still not sure of my ability to speak coherently with so many wants and needs and desires swirling inside me.

'Bene,' he said lapsing into Italian, which I knew he only did when his emotions were too close to the surface. He grabbed my glass and dumped it on the waiter's tray too, then grasped my hand. 'Because I want to get my hands on you,' he said, marching through the crowd as he hauled me towards the ballroom and the sound of the orchestra playing another waltz. 'And the only way I'm going to be able to do that for the next few hours is to dance with you.'

He spun me into his arms, his steps assured and confident, his arms holding me tight. I clung to his wide shoulders as the kaleidoscope of lights whirled around us.

My heart expanded another inch, threatening to choke

me. The dangerous emotions surging through me were so strong and so real I knew they would hurt immeasurably tomorrow when we parted—and this affair was over. But tonight all I was capable of doing was following his lead and letting those glorious, overwhelming feelings take hold. Because it was far too late to stop them.

The evening drifted past in a daze, his body wrapped around me as we danced, his hand never letting go of mine even when the music paused and he was forced to release me. He even gripped my hand during the speech he had to give and the final toasts.

The clock was ticking towards midnight, the applause still ringing in my ears when he dragged me through the crowd to charge up the staircase towards our suite.

Perhaps I should have been embarrassed. I could see the knowing looks on some of the guests' faces, the lascivious smiles on others. Every single person had to know exactly where we were going and why we were leaving the ball so abruptly. But after his passionate defence of me, the petty judgements of people like Elise Durand no longer had the power to hurt me.

I wanted him with a hunger that had been consuming me too—and I refused to be ashamed of it.

Even so, my breath caught in my lungs, my thighs quivering with anticipation, my nipples so hard they hurt when he slammed shut the door of our suite and pressed me back against the wood.

'I thought tonight would never end,' he growled, his irritation sending darts of pleasure through my system as he fumbled with the fastening of my gown. 'To hell with it,' he said, before the sound of rending fabric tore through the air.

Shock and excitement careered through my body as the exquisite gown slid to the floor, leaving me naked.

'*Dio?* Seriously?' he groaned, the feral grunt filled with outrage. 'All this time you've been wearing no underwear beneath this thing?'

'I couldn't,' I said, moaning as he captured one yearning nipple between his lips and plunged thick fingers between the slick folds of my sex. 'Nina insisted it would ruin the line of the dress.'

'I'm going to kill Nina next time I see her,' he said as I arched into his caresses. 'But first I'm going to punish you,' he added, but the teasing tone was hoarse and not remotely convincing.

'Please…' I said, circling my hips, thrusting against his hand, as his thumb found the swollen nub of my clitoris—the diabolical touch too much, and yet not nearly enough.

'Tell me what you need, *bella*,' he demanded.

'I need you,' I said, blurting out the truth, the emotion which had been holding me hostage all evening starting to strangle me.

'Anch'io ho bisogno di te...' he murmured, his voice as raw as my own now. *I need you too.*

I'd barely had time to translate the words, to grasp hold of what they might mean, before he released his erection and lifted me.

Suddenly, the immense weight of him was plunging heavily inside me, his hands gripping my buttocks to hold me up, to hold me open for him. My back thudded the door as he began to rock his hips and drive into me. My body welcomed the deep thrusts, the huge erection filling up the empty spaces inside me, sending me higher and higher. I sobbed as the orgasm raced towards me.

At last I soared on the rolling wave of pleasure pushing away all my doubts and fears until all that was left was the sweet, sublime joy of our lovemaking. As the orgasm broke over me and I heard his harsh shout of release echoing in my ear, I clung to him, wishing the moment could last for ever…

But knowing if tonight was all I could have, I would take it.

As I floated in afterglow, giddy and dazed and a little sore, stupidly close to tears, he carried me to the bed, then stripped off his clothing.

I needed to protect myself, I knew that, but I couldn't seem to find the energy or the will to do so as he gathered me against him, our naked bodies slick with sweat from the fury of our coupling.

'Are you okay?' he asked, his fingers brushing my hair back as he stared down at me with a tenderness that broke my heart. 'I didn't hurt you, did I?'

'No, of course not,' I said, confused by the edge in his voice.

'Are you sure?' he said. 'I just took you like a…' The remark was cut off, but I could hear what he hadn't said.

Like a whore.

But the edge in his voice was aimed at him, not me, I realised. I remembered the way he had talked about his mother, the bitterness and anger in his voice when he had told me she was a prostitute. But all I could hear now was regret. Then I remembered the way he had jumped to my defence earlier in the evening. And what he had said.

You're not your mother. And no one gets to judge you or insult you because of the mistakes she made. You're worth so much more than that. Do you understand?

And I wondered again why he had defended me so passionately. Was it just me he was trying to defend, or himself?

I lifted up on my elbow, to see his face in the darkness—and the wariness and tension I saw had the emotion flooding back which I had been trying so hard to qualify, and control.

'I love it when you take me like that,' I said, desperate to reassure him. *With such need, such urgency.*

I wanted to add the words but held back, scared to burden him with my feelings—when I could see he was struggling with his own.

'Okay, good,' he murmured, then swept his hand down my hair. 'Go to sleep,' he said, pressing me down until my head rested against his shoulder.

I kissed his chest, grinning at his huff of breath.

'Don't do that or I'm going to want you again,' he said, his voice strained. 'And then neither of us is going to get any sleep.'

His appetite for me sent a thrill through my body, but the feeling of closeness thrilled me more.

'Dante, can I ask you a question?' I said, the darkness, the intimacy making me bolder than I had ever been.

'Sure,' he grunted, stroking my hair. 'As long as you promise to go to sleep afterwards.'

'What did your mother do that made you hate her so?'

His breathing stilled as he tensed and I regretted the probing question, knowing I had no right to ask it. But before I could take it back he answered me.

'I told you. She was a prostitute,' he murmured, but he didn't sound bitter now, or angry; he simply sounded guarded.

'I know,' I said. 'And that must have been terrible for both of you,' I continued, wanting to understand; the life he had described to me sounded traumatic. 'But…'

'Why would it be terrible for her?' he interrupted me. 'She *chose* that life.'

'How do you know that?' I asked. 'Surely very few people choose to be prostitutes,' I added when he remained silent. 'They do it out of desperation or addiction or coercion. Are you sure she wasn't forced to make that choice?'

I said, wanting to ease his pain, because, beneath the harsh words, I could hear the ripple of insecurity.

He had given me so much in the past five days, by showing faith in me, by making me feel special and valued and important. And I wanted to do the same for him. Obviously his feelings for his mother were complex and their circumstances when he was growing up something I knew very little about. I couldn't right the wrongs she may have done him. But being a prostitute, being forced to sell yourself for money didn't make you a bad person; it didn't mean his mother hadn't loved him, any more than my mother's search for love in all the wrong places meant she hadn't loved me. People were complex, they could be weak and fickle, foolish and selfish, but there was almost always goodness in them too. And I had the strangest feeling when he spoke about his mother, he was also speaking about himself. I couldn't tell him how I felt about him. It was too soon. Too much. But I wanted him to know how special he was, regardless.

'How about we stop talking about her?' he said at last, his open palm stroking my hair in an absent caress—but I could hear the edge in his voice again, and knew I'd gone too far, I'd overstepped the mark. 'It's a real buzzkill,' he added. 'And the truth is, I don't hate her; I don't even remember her that well.'

'Okay,' I said.

'Hey?' He shifted, his knuckle nudging my chin up. 'Don't look so sad. What happened to me as a kid is so long ago it doesn't matter now.' But I could hear the hollow tone, and the deafening thunder of his heartbeat beneath my ear, and I wondered if he was lying.

But then he rolled on top of me and the stiff weight of his erection brushed my thigh. The inevitable surge of blood rushed to my core.

'And I've got something much more important to discuss,' he said, his tone husky and assured again.

He was distracting me with sex, putting emotional distance between us, the way he had done right from the start. But as his lips captured mine in a demanding kiss and he angled my hips to slide the thick erection home, I gave myself up to the physical pleasure to stem the foolish wave of sadness.

My feelings were my own to handle and control—and, however much it might hurt in the long run, I would always be grateful for these brief, beautiful moments of connection. I had the vague realisation my mother had made the same brutal bargain—to trade sex for intimacy–but, before the disturbing thought could take root, he rocked his hips and surged deep. I cried out as the muscles of my sex clamped around his thick length, milking him in the throes of another earth-shattering orgasm.

I drifted moments later on the edges of a dream, his arm tight around my shoulder as he lulled me to sleep, and for one foolish moment a wish flickered in my consciousness. If only I could find a way past the demanding, cynical, indomitable man he had become and reach the little boy beneath, then I could tell him how much he was loved, by me at least.

CHAPTER SIXTEEN

I LAY IN the darkness, staring at the ceiling cornice above my bed, and felt the weight of Edie's head on my shoulder. My sweat-soaked skin felt clammy as it dried.

She was exhausted; I'd exhausted her. We'd exhausted each other. But I wouldn't be sleeping any time soon, the adrenaline powering through my system like one of Alexi's damn racing cars, speeding around and around in circles with nowhere to go.

I'd pounded into her like a madman until I heard her sobs of release and felt her swollen flesh hold me in the grip of her orgasm. Not once, but twice.

But far worse had been what came in between, her quiet words, whispered in the darkness.

'What did your mother do that made you hate her so?'

'Surely few people choose to be prostitutes.'

Words that were just like Edie. Sweet, naïve, romantic… And sadly idealistic.

But, as much as I wanted to disregard what Edie had said, deny her defence of a woman who didn't deserve an ounce of my sympathy or hers, the conversation had left me feeling raw and exposed. And scared, dammit.

It was midnight. I needed to sleep too. It was going to be a long day tomorrow. I had to say goodbye to the guests, brief my finance team about the decisions made over the week and get the next stage of the expansion plan in motion now the new investors had been chosen.

Then I was supposed to be catching a flight to Las Vegas tomorrow night. I had a new hotel and casino complex opening there in two weeks and I wanted to oversee the inauguration.

But, as Edie shifted beside me, the events of the night kept tumbling over and over in my head.

I had planned to take her with me to Vegas. I'd already asked Nina to design a new wardrobe for the trip, had included Edie's name on the flight roster and informed my PA in Vegas that she would be joining me for all the events we had planned.

I was supposed to be telling her in a few hours' time.

But I couldn't ask her now. Because of that innocuous question, that should have been easily answered.

I didn't remember my mother, not really; I'd made sure of it. But Edie was right. I still hated her for what she had done to me.

But what I hated more was that Edie knew. That she had exposed my weakness so easily.

It shouldn't matter what Edie thought of me or didn't think of me. It shouldn't matter that she cared, but somehow it did. Because she already mattered to me more than she should.

Seeing the moisture in Edie's eyes when I had told her how furious I had been with Elise Durand on her behalf had all but crippled me.

Gratitude, affection, perhaps even love for me had shone clearly in her expression and for one agonising second I had wanted desperately to be worthy of it.

That desire had only escalated during the evening.

The dancing, when I couldn't let her out of my arms, the intensity of our lovemaking afterwards, had all been a pathetic attempt to redirect the feelings I had developed for Edie. But now as I lay in the darkness, the pearly light of a midsummer night illuminating the bedroom's furnishings, and felt the need still pulsing in my groin as I listened to her soft breathing, I knew I was kidding myself.

Just like all the lies I'd been telling myself for days about the reasons why I wanted to take her to Vegas with me. It wasn't for her bright, brilliant mind, or her sweet, lively companionship, or even the incredible way she responded to my touch, even though I had become addicted to all those things. No, it was far, far worse than that. I wanted her to come to Vegas with me because I didn't want this affair to end. Because, after only five days of having her in my bed and only a few weeks of having her in my life, I couldn't imagine what I would do without her.

I didn't want to let her go. Which was precisely why I had to.

I couldn't open myself up to those needs again, those wants.

I shuddered, despite the warmth of the room in the sultry night. The memory of cold stone, rain spattering my bare arms and legs, hands holding me, voices whispering strange words as I screamed and kicked and cried. The nightmares that had come again and again, waking me in strange beds, reminding me I was alone. I wasn't enough. I could never be enough.

I couldn't go back there again. Not ever. Not for any woman. I'd spent years getting over that night, burying that broken child so deep no one could find him, not even me. But somehow Edie had brought him out of hiding.

Which made her a threat I had to protect myself against.

As much as I hated the thought of letting Edie go, I hated the thought of being dependent on her touch, her laughter or her kindness a great deal more.

Edie was fierce and sweet, but also an innocent. She might believe she loved me but, once she discovered how cynical and disillusioned I really was, she would realise I could never love her back… And then her feelings would sour. Maybe not now, maybe not even in the next few weeks or months, but it would happen eventually, and it would hurt me… I could not afford to give her a chancc to break me—the way my mother had broken that little boy.

Edie's hand unfurled against my chest as she slept. She snuggled closer, resting her palm on my sternum, gravitating towards me even in sleep. The possessive, unconscious touch sent a shaft of longing through me and my heart slammed into my ribs.

I tried to calm the heavy erratic rhythm as I listened to the soft murmur of her breathing… And considered how to end our affair swiftly and irrevocably tomorrow while I waited for the dawn.

CHAPTER SEVENTEEN

Take a week off at Belle Rivière. You've earned it. Joe will be expecting you in Monaco on the eighteenth. Contact him if you have any concerns.
Buon viaggio!
D

I STARED AT the note from Dante that had been delivered to the suite as I packed, my hands shaking, and gulped down the ball of confusion and anguish in my throat.

Something was wrong. Very wrong. And now I was being forced to confront it.

I'd known something wasn't right as soon as I'd woken up this morning, my body aching from the intensity of Dante's lovemaking, with Dante nowhere in sight. It was the first time in five days I'd woken up without Dante's arms around me.

When I'd joined him in the breakfast room, he'd been in the middle of a phone call and had barely glanced at me. And I hadn't had a chance to speak to him since. Not properly. Not even during my private team interview after the guests had departed.

He'd informed me I was getting a two-thousand-euro bonus along with the rest of the team. I'd been hopelessly flattered and so proud. He hadn't mentioned us—I'd assumed as part of his efforts to keep our affair out of the work environment—so I'd made an effort not to mention anything personal too.

But before he'd dismissed me he'd told me he was offering me the probationary position he'd spoken about. I'd be working alongside Joseph Donnelly in the landmark casino in Monaco as a player strategy consultant—to observe the play and spot the systems the high stakes players were developing or using to gain an unfair advantage against the house. The salary was more than I had ever dreamed of earning—enough to support both me and Jude, to pay off the mortgage on Belle Rivière and undertake the estate's much needed renovations. We'd even be able to hire a small staff to help keep the place clean and well-maintained again—if I could persuade him I could do a better job of spotting the cheats than his current team.

It was more than I could have imagined in my wildest dreams. And I had been absolutely thrilled to accept the position.

But as soon as he'd outlined the job offer, in that impersonal, pragmatic tone, and the excitement had built under my breastbone, I'd known the primary reason I was so thrilled wasn't because of the amazing benefits and salary, or even the exciting challenges and opportunities the work would represent, but because he had shown such faith in me. And also because working in an important executive position in Dante's organisation would give me the chance not just to see him again, but maybe even for us to continue our affair. Or at least that's what I'd hoped.

Somewhere, deep down, I had even managed to convince myself that was one of the other reasons he had offered me the job. Because he wanted to keep me close too.

In the hours after I'd accepted the job and signed the contract though, there had still been no chance to talk to

Dante privately. I'd tried to convince myself it was because he was busy.

After the last of the guests had left and the team interviews had been completed, Dante had hosted a final lunch for the team out on the terrace, with everyone laughing and toasting each other on a job well done. I'd left a seat for him next to me, but he'd walked past it and taken a seat at the far end of the table with Joseph Donnelly and his events manager, Evan Jones. I'd been stupidly hurt at first and then realised how ridiculous I was being.

What was I, five? He probably still had work to discuss with Joe and Evan.

But after the meal he'd disappeared again. And my insecurities had begun to mount.

Why had he hardly spoken to me? Was he avoiding me? Was it because of what I'd said to him about his mother the night before? Why had I probed like that?

I'd tried to keep a lid on my fears and anxieties by keeping busy myself. Surely he would talk to me in time, explain what was happening, where we stood.

After saying goodbye to the other team members as they climbed into their various cars and taxis, I had headed up to our suite of rooms. The vague hope I'd had that he might be up there packing had been dashed when I'd walked in on a maid busy folding all his clothes into a series of suitcases.

I'd duly packed my own stuff. At last there had been nothing else left to do, I could hear the staff being ordered about by Collette, who was making the final preparations to clear the chateau and close it up for the next few weeks. As I sat in the bedroom alone, my own suitcases stacked ready to leave, I began to feel as if I had been totally forgotten. Should I go downstairs, find Dante? Where was he? Was it possible he'd already left, without even telling me?

And that's when one of Dante's assistants had come to

inform me Dante had arranged for the company helicopter to return me to Belle Rivière. And handed me the note, written in Dante's bold cursive script.

I read it again as my head started to pound.

Had he dismissed me? The chill that had been working its way over my skin all day seemed to wrap around my heart.

Had I done something wrong? Was it because of the liberties I'd taken last night? Was he angry about that conversation? What had happened to the man who had been prepared to fight for my honour over a single snide comment? Who had danced with me and then made love to me—bringing me to two mind-blowing orgasms. And then held me in his arms while I fell asleep.

I didn't understand; my confusion became almost as huge as the deep well of hurt at his actions.

Was this how my mother had always felt? When she'd been discarded by the men she had loved.

I'd tried to tell myself my affair with Dante was not the same, because I was working for him. Because we were equals. Because I hadn't become too invested in our relationship. But as the empty space in my belly grew, seeming to consume me, I knew that was a lie.

Something fundamental had changed for me last night. And it hadn't changed for him. Or he wouldn't have ignored me today.

I wanted to feel outraged, but all I felt was devastated.

I folded the note.

'Do you want to leave now?' the young man who had delivered the note said. 'I believe the helicopter is ready whenever you want to go.'

'Is Dant… I mean, is Mr Allegri still here?' I asked.

I should leave—a part of me knew it would only hurt more to confront him about my dismissal. I wouldn't make a scene, I promised myself, remembering all those times I'd heard my mother plead, or seen her cling to a lover as he'd left her. Remembering the times my sister and I had crept into her bed and tried to comfort her tears, tried to stave off the black mood we knew would come until she found a new 'protector'. I wouldn't do that. I couldn't.

My heart wasn't broken. I couldn't let it be. I couldn't afford to lose the job he'd offered me.

He owed me nothing; I understood that. I'd entered into this affair with my eyes open. Or at least I had tried to. And, while things had changed for me, it wasn't his fault that they hadn't changed for him. It had only been five days after all. Five glorious, intense days. But I couldn't live with myself if I didn't at least get to say goodbye.

Before I saw him again in a work situation I needed to have closure. To know that there was no chance for us, or I might become delusional again.

The young man smiled. 'Yes, he's still here; he's in his office.'

'Do you know if he's with anyone?' I asked. I wanted to be brave and bold, the way he'd made me feel this past week, but I wasn't quite bold or brave enough to interrupt him while he was in a meeting.

'No, everyone else has left except you and the skeleton staff who are locking up the villa.'

I nodded and stood up. 'If you could have the luggage taken to the helicopter, that would be great. I'll meet you down there.' I would need to make a quick getaway once I'd said my goodbyes. I couldn't afford to linger, or the boulder pressing against my larynx might start to choke me.

The young man nodded and left to get some of the staff to help him.

I tucked the curt, businesslike note into the back pocket of my jeans, brushed sweaty palms on the denim and headed in the opposite direction. As I approached Dante's office, my throat started to ache with unshed tears. I'd been such a naïve fool.

I didn't knock. I didn't have to; his office door was ajar and I could see him sitting at his desk, tapping on his laptop. He was wearing the same shirt and tailored trousers combo he'd worn when I'd come in here for my interview.

His head jerked up as I stepped into the room, reminding me painfully of the first time we'd made love—the way he'd sensed my presence while he'd stood on the beach.

His eyes narrowed. 'Edie, hello—is there a problem with the travel arrangements?' he asked. 'I thought you would have left by now.'

So polite. So distant. So businesslike. How could this be the same man who had plunged into me over and over again—as if he wanted to brand me as his?

'I wanted to say goodbye before I left,' I said. 'I thought…' The words jammed in my throat as he continued to look at me as if I were just another employee.

He closed his laptop and leaned back in his chair. 'You thought what?' he said, not unkindly, but the whisper of impatience in his tone destroyed me.

'I thought… I didn't think it would end like this.'

'How did you think it would end?' he said, confirming my worst fears—that this was it, that he had tired of me, that I had been discarded.

The man in front of me looked like Dante Allegri. He had the same striking bone structure, the same muscular physique. I could see the tattoo that looped around his shoulder peeking through the open collar of his shirt. I noticed the small scar on his top lip. But this wasn't the man who had held me last night. Because that man had been arrogant, yes, and more than a little domineering, but he hadn't been cruel.

'I thought you would have told me…' I said, trying to keep my voice firm, so as not to give away how devastated I was.

'I was busy today, Edie,' he said, and it occurred to me that he hadn't once called me *bella*, not since last night. Not since the last time we had made love. 'I simply didn't have time.'

'You didn't have time to even speak to me?' I said, incredulous now as well as devastated.

'We did speak—I offered you a very lucrative contract and you accepted it, as I recall.'

'Is it because of what I said about your mother? I know it was none of my business and I'm so sorry…' I began realising I was begging after all when he held up his hand.

'Of course not,' he said. 'If you're going to make an emotional scene now though, I may have to reconsider my offer. I know you're young and naïve but I got the impression you understood exactly where this was leading.'

The chill spread through me at the curt tone. He was talking to me as if I were a child.

'But I…'

'*You* came to *me*, Edie, if you recall. You made it clear you wanted me as a lover. If you now feel you gave away your virginity too cheaply, I'm afraid it's too late to change your mind.'

I trembled, the blood exploding in my ears, the caustic, casual tone almost as agonising as the contempt on his face.

'You… You knew?' I gasped, shock warring with devastation.

He leaned forward. 'Of course I knew. I'm not quite as inexperienced as you are.'

'But you didn't say anything?' I said, still unable to grasp why he seemed angry about it.

'Why would I? It was none of my concern,' he said,

but I could still hear it in his voice, that edge of steel, the accusation. And then the rest of his comment came back to me, hitting me in the solar plexus with the force of a sledgehammer.

If you now feel you gave away your virginity too cheaply.

And I realised what he was accusing me of. Of trying to trick him, to deceive him, to make him feel beholden to me, to barter my body for money. When I had never once put any demands on him. Even now all I'd asked for was a proper goodbye.

'I didn't expect anything in return,' I said. 'I gave myself to you freely. I wanted you to be my first.' I tried to explain, the words tumbling over themselves, struggling to get out of my mouth in the face of his cynicism. 'Why would you even think that?' I asked, horrified anew at the accusation and the cool scepticism on his face.

'All sex is a transaction,' he said. 'Of one form or another. Your mother knew it, and so did mine.'

'That's not true. My mother always loved the men she slept with…' I said, my heart shattering in my chest. This wasn't just scepticism; this was damage. How could he believe the things he was saying? What had happened to him that would make him so hard, so cold, so uncaring and so cynical? He'd said he didn't hate his mother, but now I could see he'd lied.

'How convenient then, that she only ever fell in love with rich men,' he said, the mockery in his voice reminding me of all the times I had been teased or insulted, made to feel less than, an outcast, because of the way people judged my mother.

But this was so much worse.

Tears stung the backs of my eyes, tears I knew I couldn't shed. I'd thought he'd understood. That he'd been on my side. But he was worse than any of them.

'You bastard,' I whispered, trying to locate the anger I should be feeling to cover the misery.

'We're both bastards, Edie. I thought we already established that.'

'I'm not talking about the circumstances of your birth. You… You used me,' I said, still not able to believe it.

'We used each other. You amused me this week, and I gave you the chance to discover what a sensual person you are. Something that you've clearly been denying, or you wouldn't have remained a virgin so long.'

I nodded. 'Well, thanks for that,' I said, trying to sound flippant, trying to wound him the way he'd wounded me. 'I'll be sure to use the lessons you taught me about how to pleasure a man when I take my next lover.'

His jaw tightened, his brows lowering in a thunderous frown as I turned and fled.

It wasn't until I was sitting in the helicopter, the blades whirring, the sun dipping towards the horizon as the huge black machine lifted into the sky, that I finally let the tears fall. Tears of anguish, and grief. And humiliation at my own stupidity. But, most of all, tears of heartache—which only made the humiliation worse.

How could I ever have been young enough or naïve enough to be fooled by Dante Allegri—to have believed that, buried beneath the ambition and the ruthlessness, the magnetism and the overpowering sexuality and the horrors he had obviously suffered as a child, there lay a kindred spirit, a man who, despite everything, had a good heart?

I gulped down my sobs and scrubbed the tears off my cheeks, forcing my gaze away from the villa and towards the horizon.

I would survive and I would prosper. I would be the best employee he'd ever had. And I would be grateful for the important lesson he had taught me. A lesson I thought I had learned during the years of my childhood.

Never to fall in love with a man who valued money and power and ambition—for whatever reason—over love.

CHAPTER EIGHTEEN

'Is that Edie, talking to Alexi Galanti?' I barked at Joe Donnelly who had greeted me at the entrance to The Inferno as I spotted Edie's slim figure displayed in a wisp of blue silk standing beside the Formula One owner on the far corner of the casino floor.

Anxiety and anger sliced through my gut. I'd stayed away from Monaco for three weeks. Three long torturous weeks. As memories of Edie and what we'd shared tormented me daily.

Her face, determined and tense on our first night together, as she played poker. Her lips, trembling but eager, as I kissed her in the moonlight. Her breasts, full and yearning, in that excuse for a bikini. Her arms soft and secure as we danced together at the investors' ball. Her eyes, the deep green sheened with tears, as I forced her to accept the reality of who I was and how little I could offer her.

Every one of those memories slammed into me now as I stared at her like a starving man. Memories that had turned my temper into gelignite, ready to explode at a moment's notice. Memories that bombarded me every time I closed my eyes. Then woke me up, hard and aching and empty inside. Memories which were the real reason I'd arrived in Monaco unannounced. Because after three weeks of staying away, of trying and failing to forget about her, I hadn't. And now this is what I found.

The woman I'd initiated, looking at another man the way she'd once looked at me.

'Yeah, Edie's hosting the Millionaire Club game tonight; Alexi's playing.' Joe's voice murmured beside me but I could barely hear it through the buzzing in my brain.

Why was she smiling at Alexi like that? Was there something between them? Why hadn't I listened to my instincts and returned sooner? She was an innocent and I'd let her loose among a sea of sharks. My friend—or, rather, my former friend—being the most voracious and ruthless of the lot.

'Nice to see you too, by the way,' Joe said, curtly enough to distract me for a second. 'We weren't expecting to see you for another week.'

'My plans changed,' I said, turning back to stare at the woman who had haunted my dreams. Alexi was standing too damn close to her. I didn't like it. Any more than I liked the low neckline on her dress. He could probably see right down to her navel in that thing.

Joe's fingers clicked in my face. 'Snap out of it, Dante.'

'What?' I forced my eyes away.

'You're staring at her as if you want to devour her in a few quick greedy bites.'

Because I do.

I wetted my lips, trying to deny the errant thought as blood surged heavily into my groin.

'Alexi's got no damn business hovering around her like that. She's an employee here.'

'I know that,' Joe said, searching my face in a way I didn't like. 'But do you?'

'What's that supposed to mean?'

'You know damn well what it means,' he shot back, only

increasing my irritation. Joe was a friend, probably my best friend. He'd been my wingman since we were little more than kids. But no one got to speak to me like that, not even him. Before I could point this out though, he cut me off.

'You've been ringing me every day to check up on her. And now you're here, when you're supposed to be in Paris. What the hell is going on between you two, because I thought you broke up with her?'

'Alexi's flirting with my employee and I'm not supposed to be pissed about that?' I said, raising my voice as my gaze locked on Edie again across the casino.

Damn, but I had missed her. The sight of her, the smell of her, the feel of her body curled around me in sleep. When was this longing going to end? Why couldn't I get a handle on it? And why did seeing her again only make all the memories worse, not better, the way I'd hoped?

'Alexi flirts with everyone,' Joe said, raising his voice too. 'It never bothered you before.'

We were starting to attract attention. But then Alexi lifted his finger to tuck a lock of hair behind Edie's ear. And Edie smiled at him, that sweet smile that had only ever been meant for me.

Rage exploded inside me, the same rage I had kept so carefully at bay… Ever since Edie had thrown her parting words at me.

I'll be sure to use the lessons you taught me about how to pleasure a man when I take my next lover.

Those words had tortured me every night since. But I'd stayed away, determined not to give in to the need, the jealousy, the longing.

Big mistake.

'Bastardo!' I shouted and several people turned towards me.

'Dante, wait!' Joe said, trying to grab my arm, I shook it off as I strode through the crowd.

This ended here and now. Edie needed to protect herself against guys like Alexi Galanti. She was too innocent and naïve—what the hell had I been thinking, giving her a job that would expose her to bastards like him? And then left her alone. She needed my protection, now more than ever. Even if we weren't together, I had a responsibility to keep her safe.

As I approached, Edie's head swung round as if she had sensed my approach. The deep emerald gaze which had always captivated me locked with mine. My stride faltered, the jolt of awareness hitting me like a bolt of lightning as our eyes met.

'Dante?' Her lips slicked with gloss whispered my name—and I heard it in my soul.

'Galanti, you're banned,' I snarled at Alexi without taking my gaze off Edie.

I shoved him aside, grasped Edie's arm and carried on walking, marching her towards the security booth at the back of the casino. Her skin felt so soft, so fragile beneath my fingertips. Her biceps tensed and I loosened my fingers, scared to hurt her, but kept my grip firm, knowing I never wanted to let her go.

Alexi shouted something after us—mocking or annoyed—I couldn't tell because of the blood rushing in my ears. But I didn't care because all I could see was Edie, and all I could feel was the surge of heat shooting up my arm and the rage threatening to blow the top of my head off.

'Why are you here?' she said, confused, wary, wounded, but she didn't resist me as I dragged her into the booth. 'Have I done something wrong?'

'We need to talk,' I said, struggling to keep my voice

firm and even. 'Everyone out,' I shouted at the three guys in the booth.

The security personnel scurried out, leaving us alone as I forced myself to release her arm and kicked the door shut. The blue light from the monitors illuminated her face. How could I have forgotten how exquisite she was? With her hair gathered in some kind of up-do, the tendrils caressed her neck. Her full breasts rose and fell in staggered rhythm against the revealing bodice of that excuse for a gown. The desire to bury my face against her neck and breathe in her fresh, sultry scent, to lick her collarbone and gather her taste on my tongue, to tear off her gown so I could free those ripe orbs, capture her nipples in my teeth and…

Focus, Dante. Dio!

I shook my head, trying to clear the erotic fog that descended whenever I was near her. I wasn't here to slake my own hunger. I was here to protect her from guys like Alexi Galanti… And myself.

'Are you sleeping with him?' I asked, the words coming out on a hoarse rasp of breath as a sense of loss and injustice wrapped around my heart. I'd given her up to save her from me. And she'd immediately been seduced by a man who was just as jaded and cynical as I was. If not more so.

I should have come to check up on her in person a lot sooner. I'd given her this position to keep her safe, to keep her secure, to keep an eye on her. And then I'd stayed away from her. What a damn fool I'd been.

But I was here now, and I wasn't leaving again until she understood I would do whatever I had to do to protect her. Even if it meant protecting her from her own naiveté.

'Because he's not worthy of you, *bella*,' I added. 'Any more than I am.'

She was staring at me, her face flaming with the delectable blush which marked out her innocence. She might think she was experienced, worldly, because of what we'd shared, but she wasn't. She was far too gullible, too innocent, too idealistic to ever understand the way men's minds worked.

'Answer me, *bella*,' I said, steeling myself against her answer as I cupped her cheek. She jerked away from my touch and the knife twisted in my gut. 'Are you sleeping with Alexi?'

CHAPTER NINETEEN

'WHY DO YOU want to know that?' I whispered at the man in front of me as emotions I'd struggled to keep in check for weeks threatened to destroy me all over again.

The giddy rush of love I still couldn't control had risen up as soon as I'd spotted him striding towards me—even in black jeans and a dark polo shirt he had looked indomitable, overwhelming, as the casino patrons in tuxedos and evening gowns scattered to let him pass—but right behind that rush of love had been the shattering pain he'd caused.

I clasped my arms around my waist, trying to hold in the violent trembling as conflicting emotions swelled and surged inside me. Shock, panic, confusion, desire, love, longing, but most of all the deep, dark well of hurt that had dogged me ever since the last time I'd seen him.

I stared at him now, trying to understand. But he looked like a madman—his breathing ragged, his chest heaving, his eyes wild with something I didn't understand.

And while a million questions swirled in my head, about what he was doing here, why he was behaving like this and what any of it had to do with Mr Galanti, the only one I could grasp was one I had asked myself a thousand times since the last time I'd seen him.

How could he look at me with such longing when he had discarded me so easily? It had taken me three weeks to convince myself it hadn't been my fault. I shouldn't have spoken to him about his mother, I could see that, but I hadn't meant to upset him. Maybe what I'd said had been misguided, inappropriate, but it had come from a place of love.

'I need to know if Alexi has seduced you?' he said, his voice surprisingly firm for someone who appeared to be talking in tongues. 'Because if he has I'm going to kill him.'

'Stop it,' I hissed, my lungs tight with all those conflicting emotions now. 'Stop asking me about Mr Galanti—are you mad?'

'Mr Galanti? Not Alexi. *Grazie a Dio.*' He let out a relieved chuckle, the self-satisfied slash of white in his tanned face making him look like a marauding pirate to my confused mind. 'So you haven't slept with him.'

His blue eyes lit with determination and danger as he lifted his hand and touched his thumb to the rampaging pulse in my collarbone.

'This is good news, *bella*. I am proud of you.'

The tidal wave of longing hit me hard, spreading heat throughout my body. The desire to lean in to the caress, to accept his praise, his protection, almost more than I could bear. Hadn't I dreamt about this happening every night since I'd left La Villa Paradis? That he would come back, that he would claim me, that he would tell me he still cared about me, that one day he might take me back. That he hadn't meant to destroy me the way he had.

But what hit me harder was the tidal wave of fury. The fury I'd tried so hard to locate three weeks ago when he'd dumped me—because his behaviour then hadn't been a mistake. It had been callous and deliberate and unnecessarily brutal.

Fury spread through my body like wildfire, torching everything in its wake—the yearning, the confusion, the anguish, the hollow empty loneliness, the weeks of soul-searching and recriminations—until all that was left was the burning desire to hurt him the way he'd hurt me.

I slapped at his hand, hard enough to make him grunt.

'Don't you dare touch me,' I yelled. 'How dare you ask me about my sex life...? You...' I was so furious I could barely speak. 'You have no right.'

'I have every right,' he barked back, but I could see my outburst had shocked him—almost as much as it had shocked me. 'You're my employee,' he said, but for once he didn't sound sure or indomitable. Instead he sounded tense and wary. 'And I was your first lover. I'm trying to protect you. Alexi is a notorious playboy. He uses women and then he discards them, he...'

'This has nothing to do with Mr Galanti,' I interrupted him, finally finding the words I should have found three weeks ago. 'And don't you dare throw my virginity back in my face again. If I was ever innocent I'm certainly not any more. And if you wanted to protect me, why didn't you protect me from you, Dante?' I pointed out, just in case he'd forgotten that salient point.

Tears rolled down my cheeks and I scrubbed them away, but I wasn't ashamed of them any more and I wasn't afraid to let him see them.

'*Bella*, please don't cry,' he said in an agonised whisper and reached for me again. But I stepped back.

'No,' I said, firmly and succinctly, even though my heart was ripping open inside my chest. 'You *left* me, Dante. Which means you don't get to come storming back into my life three weeks later, telling me who I can and cannot sleep with. You don't get to call me *bella*, or touch me as if you own me, or look at me as if you care about me when we both know you don't. You *hurt* me,' I said, my breath shuddering out as the tears mercifully stopped. 'I know it was only five days. I know I overreacted, probably romanticised it too much. That it was too soon. But those feelings were still real. I was falling in love with you and you knew… And still you treated me like nothing.'

'You were an innocent. I only discarded you to protect you,' he said, his voice raw with emotion now too, and I could see he actually believed it—which only made the heartache worse.

'No, you didn't,' I said, the tears still lodged in my throat as I realised how hopeless this situation was and had always been. He still wanted me and I still wanted him—we could have had so much, could have built on those five glorious days together—but it wasn't my insecurities that had held us back, as a part of me had always believed—it was his. 'You did it to protect yourself,' I said.

I clasped my arms around my waist to control the trembles threatening to tear me apart.

'I don't know what your mother did to you, Dante,' I said and he stiffened, his eyes becoming shadowed and distant, as I hit the raw nerve I knew would always lie between us. 'But, whatever it is,' I said, 'I hope one day you can get over it.'

I walked past him. I had to get out of here, to get away from him. It had been a mistake taking this job. I'd done it for all the wrong reasons. I'd wanted to be able to see him again, to be near him, even if he didn't want me any more. I'd wanted the chance to impress him, to soak up his approval. I had convinced myself in the last three weeks my susceptibility to Dante's charms had been a result of the skewed legacy of being my mother's daughter, being fatherless—that I had an unconscious need for male attention I had never acknowledged before. But I realised now it was more personal than that… And the mistakes made had been his as much as mine. He was right, I had been innocent and naïve and maybe too gullible. He'd been my first lover and my first love—and he was an overpowering man. But he had used me, and it was way past time I protected myself against him and the overwhelming effect he had on me.

'Where are you going?' he demanded. 'You're still my employee.'

'Not any more,' I said. 'I quit.'

CHAPTER TWENTY

'YOU NEED TO go get her back, Dante. Apologise, grovel, do whatever you have to do, but we need her here.'

'No,' I said calmly to Joe, even though calm was the last thing I felt.

'Why not?' My casino manager leaned forward in the chair on the other side of my desk, about to launch into the diatribe I'd been hearing for three days now, ever since Edie had walked out of the casino, still wearing the dress I'd bought her. The dress had been returned a day later, along with the rest of the wardrobe I'd ordered from Nina Saint Jus—but she hadn't.

The grinding pain in the pit of my stomach, that deep well of emptiness and guilt which had only got bigger since our showdown in the booth, grew another few centimetres.

'Because there's no point in apologising,' I said.

'Of course there is,' Joe said. 'You behaved like a dick. If you...'

'It's not that I *won't* apologise; it's that it would do no good,' I clarified, feeling unbearably weary. I'd had three more sleepless nights since Edie had walked away from me. But this time, instead of hot, sweaty dreams of Edie, my nights had been filled with cold, rain-spattered nightmares—the same nightmares that had haunted me throughout my childhood. My mother's face, sad and pleading. My childish terror as it had dawned on me that she was never coming back.

The questions that had tormented me then had woken me in a cold sweat in the middle of the night.

Why wasn't I enough? Why hadn't she loved me? Why had she abandoned me?

But this time the answer had been all too obvious.

Edie had abandoned me because I was a selfish coward. I'd been too scared to reach for the golden ring, had refused to trust my feelings and hers, because of something that had happened over twenty years ago. Edie had called it exactly right. I had discarded her to protect myself and this was the inevitable result. I'd destroyed what we might have had, only to realise what it was I'd lost when it was way too late to get it back.

'That's nuts!' Joe said. 'She needs this job—she's got a mortgage to pay. And she's brilliant at it. If you just tell her you'll never behave like a dick again she…'

'I can't do that either,' I said, the hopelessness of the situation suffocating me as I met Joe's accusing gaze. 'Because I can't guarantee I won't act like that again. I can't be rational where she's concerned. Seeing her with Alexi made me behave like a crazy person. Just thinking about her with another man is tying my guts in knots right now.' Yet another cross I was going to have to bear for a long time to come.

Joe's eyes widened. He swore softly in Irish. 'I had no idea you'd fallen in love with her.' He slumped in his chair, finally realising the hopelessness of the situation too. 'In less than a week. That's a hell of a thing.'

I let out a humourless laugh. *'Precisamente.'*

How ironic that it didn't even freak me out to admit how far gone I was over Edie.

Less than a month ago—hell, only three days ago—I

would have laughed in Joe's face if he'd suggested such a thing to me. I would have called him a romantic fool. A gullible, naïve idiot—which is what I'd accused Edie of being.

I hadn't believed in love, then. Hadn't believed it really existed. And, if it did, I had considered it a weakness, a foolish sentimental emotion to be avoided and denied until it went away.

'I can't believe she walked out of here after you told her,' Joe said. 'I could have sworn she felt the same way. She was gutted after you broke up with her at the Villa, even though she was doing her best to hide it, poor kid.'

The shaft of guilt, fuelled by the memory of the tears streaming down her cheeks in the booth, combined with the hole in the pit of my stomach to make it a yawning chasm.

I know it was only five days. I know I overreacted, probably romanticised it too much. That it was too soon. But those feelings were still real. I was falling in love with you and you knew... And still you treated me like nothing.

'I didn't tell her,' I corrected Joe as the evidence of exactly how badly I'd treated her echoed in my head.

'Why not?' Joe looked dumbfounded.

'Because I'd already hurt her too much.'

What would be the point of telling her I loved her when she would never be able to forgive me? When I couldn't even forgive myself?

'That sounds like an excuse to me,' Joe said. 'How do you know what she'd do if you didn't even tell her how you feel about her? Isn't that making the choice for her?'

Something built under my breastbone, fuelled by the conviction in Joe's tone.

'I don't want to hurt her any more than I already have,' I said, but my reasoning sounding weak even to me.

Could Joe be right? Was there still a chance?

'I don't see how telling her you love her is gonna hurt her,' he said bluntly.

But what if she decides she doesn't want me?

The real reason I was reluctant to go to her, to lay my feelings bare, reverberated in my head. It was the same fear that had haunted me my whole life. What if I took this chance, risked everything, and she rejected me? Edie had the power to wound me in ways no other woman had—since my mother.

Except Edie wasn't my mother. She hadn't abandoned me. Until I'd abandoned her.

Images of her—in her second-hand ballgown playing poker to save her home, with a bruise blossoming on her cheek as she defended herself against a thug, with tears streaming down her cheeks as she stood up to me—shimmered across my consciousness.

Edie was brave and tough, passionate and resourceful and strong. She'd taken terrible risks, defied impossible odds to protect her family and her home. Perhaps it was time I did the same… If I wanted to be worthy of her.

CHAPTER TWENTY-ONE

'EDIE, AT LAST you're back. Didn't you get any of my texts?' my sister greeted me as I dumped my bag of cleaning supplies on the hall floor.

'I had a job to do, Jude,' I said, stretching my back to work out the kinks that had set in after scrubbing what felt like an acre of parquet flooring. 'I can't answer my phone while I'm working. If anyone catches me, they think I'm slacking.'

Walking out of my job at the casino had been the right thing to do. I would never get a handle on my feelings for Dante if I remained in his orbit. But having to return to scrubbing floors for a living had felt like an additional punishment I didn't deserve.

'There's someone here to see you. He's waiting in the library,' Jude said.

'Who?'

'Mr Allegri,' she said, triggering the myriad emotions I'd been trying to suppress. 'I think he wants to offer you your job back.' She sounded so pleased and eager I didn't have the heart to tell her the truth.

I hadn't explained any of it to Jude. That I'd fallen in love with a man as damaged and ruthless as the men our mother had always gravitated towards.

'I don't want to see him.' I couldn't speak to him now,

whatever he had to say to me. It would hurt too much to hash over it all again. And I couldn't be sure that I would stick to my guns. That I had the strength to walk away a second time.

But Jude had already grasped my arm and was tugging me towards the library. 'Don't be daft, Edie. You have to see him. He came all the way here in his helicopter. And he looks… I don't know…he looks a little desperate.'

Before I could muster the strength to tell her the truth, she had propelled me into the room, run out and slammed the door shut behind her.

'Edie?' Dante appeared out of the shadows in the room, which was lit by a single lamp in the corner.

The sight of his tall frame and broad shoulders had a predictable effect on me. I tried to stifle it, to stay strong. I'd thought it all through. I'd fallen into the same trap as my mother by falling for this man. But if I could just stay away from him, I'd get over it eventually.

'You have to leave, Dante,' I said. 'I can't come back to the casino, if that's why you're here.' I'd done a good job, I knew that—which was probably why he had come. He was a practical, pragmatic businessman, and I'd managed to spot three cheats at the high stakes game in as many weeks.

'I'm not here about the job. I have one simple question to ask you.' He walked towards me. 'Do you love me? If you do, it is not too late.'

Desperation assailed me at the intensity in his gaze. I shook my head. I wanted to tell him no. I wanted for it not to be true. How could I still be so besotted with a man who had hurt me? But I couldn't say the words and I saw the spark of hope light his eyes.

'Tell me you don't still love me and I will go, *bella*,' he said. 'And we will never speak of this again.'

A part of me hated him in that moment. Because I knew

he would see right through the lie if I tried to deny my feelings for him. But it was so grossly unfair, that I should be bound by my emotions, tricked into giving in to him when it would make me so vulnerable again.

Unable to speak, I turned to flee from the room.

But he followed me, flattening his palm against the door as I tried to open it. I stood in the cage of his arms, pressing my forehead to the worn wood, feeling my body succumb to desire—as it always did when he was near me. I could smell him, the tempting scent of salt and cedar and musk assaulting my nostrils as he stood too close behind me.

'You cannot say it, *bella*, because it is true,' he whispered against my neck. 'You love me and you still want me, you know you do. Let me make it better. Let me fix this.'

I swung round and flattened my palms against his chest. He was going to kiss me. He wanted to kiss me. I could see the yearning in his face because it matched my own. But I found the strength from somewhere to hold him off.

'Don't you see it isn't enough?' I said. To my surprise, instead of taking advantage of my weakness, he let his arms fall and stepped back.

'It doesn't matter if I love you,' I added, suddenly weary to the bone. 'It doesn't matter if I still want you. If I let you kiss me now, make love to me again, after the way you treated me, I'd simply be inviting you to do it again. I saw my mother eventually become a shadow of herself that way. Each time a new love affair started she would kid herself that this man would be different. She did everything in her power to make those men love her, but of course they didn't because she was too compliant, too undemanding, too accommodating. She never asked for a commitment, for an equal stake in those relationships and, because she didn't, they eventually grew bored of her, the way you grew bored of me.'

'I never grew bored of you…' he interrupted, his voice breaking now too. 'I wanted you so much. I still do.' His gaze roamed over me, the look of need in his eyes open and unguarded for the first time since I'd met him.

'You're just talking about sex,' I said, despairing.

'No, that isn't it,' he said, the fervour in his voice fierce and uninhibited. 'I didn't just want you in my bed. I wanted you to be a part of my life.' He sighed. 'Your wit, your joy, your kindness, your intelligence—everything about you turns me on, not just your delectable body.'

He lifted his hand as if to touch me, but then dropped it when I flinched.

'It's why I couldn't stay away from you. Why I went insane when I saw you talking to Alexi. I am in love with you too, *bella*. Please tell me it's not too late to make this right.'

His words crucified me, because I could hear the truth in them. He was serious. But I forced myself to stifle the hope that wanted to surge through me. Because it still wasn't enough. In fact it was almost worse.

If he had fallen for me too, how could he have hurt me the way he had? And what was going to stop him from doing it again?

'How could you treat me that way if you loved me?' I asked.

He let out a heavy sigh and I could see the turmoil in his face, but I couldn't let it go. I deserved an answer.

'Because loving you terrified me,' he murmured.

The clouds passed over the moon as he said it and the silvery light shone through the library window, illuminating his face which had been thrown into shadow by the lamp behind him. For the first time, I saw circles under his eyes and the tight lines around his mouth. He was exhausted, I realised.

I wanted to cradle his cheeks in my palms, to hold him

close and promise him that whatever demons were chasing him, I would scare them away… But I fisted my fingers and kept my hands by my sides. If I gave in to the urge to soothe and comfort him, I might never know why he had reacted the way he had, and then I would be the one who was scared—scared it could happen again.

'What were you terrified of?' I asked.

His gaze flashed with emotions so real and vulnerable my heart contracted in my chest, my breath squeezing out of my lungs.

'That you would leave me,' he said, the words so low I could barely hear them above the ambient sounds of the night outside the library window, the hum of the crickets and the rustle of the forest leaves. 'The way she did.'

'Is this your mother?' I asked.

I saw his Adam's apple bob. Then he nodded. 'When you asked me about her, I lied. I said I didn't remember her. But the truth is, when I began to have feelings for you…it all came back to me. What happened that day. And I was scared it would happen again,' he said.

He looked away, but I had seen the naked pain in his face. My heart lurched in my chest. He had pushed me away because he was scared of losing me. As mad as that sounded on one level, it made complete sense to me on another.

I cupped his cheek, drew his head round to mine, unable to hold back a moment longer. I felt the muscles in his jaw bunch as I kissed him softly. His breath brushed my cheek as he sighed.

'Can you tell me what happened?' I asked.

He touched his forehead to mine, placed his hands on my hips to draw me into his arms, but I could hear the hopelessness in his voice when he said, 'Yes.'

CHAPTER TWENTY-TWO

IF ONLY I could avoid this conversation. I'd spent so much of my life denying what had happened to me. How could the wounds still be so raw, so fresh? But I knew I owed it to Edie. How would she ever be able to trust me again after what I had done, if I didn't explain why I had done it?

I'd tried to dodge and avoid, but she'd been brave and determined. And now I needed to be brave too.

'I was maybe five, six, I can't remember.' I started to talk as I clung to her, breathing in her scent to give me strength, and balance—as I tumbled into the black hole of memory. 'The night before, there had been…violence. Her pimp had beaten her. I had tried to intervene and he had beaten me too…'

Edie shuddered with reaction, her hands settling on my lower back, keeping me upright. 'It's okay,' she said. 'I'm here.'

It was exactly the right thing to say. It grounded me, reminded me that I wasn't that little boy any more, so scared, so brutalised. I was a grown man, and Edie would never hurt me the way my mother had.

'I think maybe that was the reason she wanted to get rid of me. She cried a lot the next morning. Then she made me dress in my best clothes and took me to the steps of the church where we went to Mass each Sunday.' I huffed out a bitter laugh. 'Ironic, no? That a prostitute would go to church?'

'Go on,' Edie said.

'She told me to wait for her, that she would be back soon. She told me that she loved me before she left me there.' The bitterness sharpened as I recalled her exact words, and the quiver of emotion in her voice as she whispered the lie in my ear.

'Coraggio, Dante. Ti voglio bene assai.'

Be a brave boy, Dante. I love you very much.

'I waited, as people came and went. The priest tried to talk to me and then a policeman and a social worker came. It had begun to rain and they wanted me to come inside the church. I went wild. I told them I couldn't go inside, that I mustn't leave. I was sure that she would come back because she had promised me she would. And I was scared that if I left that step she would never find me.' I shook, remembering the tears again, the screams, the rain cold and clammy on my skin, the grunts of the policeman as I kicked against his hold.

'Oh, Dante, I'm so sorry.' Edie's arms closed around me and she held me tight, burying her head against my chest. I could feel her tears dampening my shirt. But her anguish didn't feel like pity any more; it felt like compassion. 'It must have been so agonising for you,' she said, her words muffled, 'and for her.'

The last part of her sentence struck me and I drew back, all the emotion I had locked away for so long coalescing in the pit of my stomach and plunging into the black hole.

'Why would it be hard for her?' I asked, but the emotion welling in my throat felt strange and different this time, not jagged and ugly, just weary and tense. 'She didn't love me. She abandoned me.'

Edie lifted her face from my chest. 'Do you really think so?'

'Of course,' I said, but the doubt in her voice gave me pause.

'What happened to you afterwards? After she left you?' Edie asked.

'I went into the foster system in Naples. I found it hard to settle. I was so lonely. I wanted my mother. And then I became angry. That she had left me.'

'But were you ever hit again? Or abused?' she asked.

'No,' I said. If anything, I was the one who had been abusive, I realised, as I remembered the many families who had taken me in. Hard-working, good people, who had only wanted to help me and whose help I had rejected.

'Do you think it's possible that she left you there not because she didn't love you, but because she loved you very much? And she didn't want to see you hurt again? Her lifestyle sounds as if it was very chaotic; maybe she was trying to protect you?' Her voice was coaxing and gentle and devoid of criticism—but still I could hear the truth in it when she said, 'You said she had a pimp who was violent. Isn't it possible she thought she had to give you up to keep you safe?'

Something snapped open deep inside me at Edie's comment. And suddenly all the memories I had kept locked away in my subconscious for years burst out.

'Ti voglio bene assai.'

How often had my mother said those words to me? Not just that one time, but a hundred times. A thousand? How often had she hugged me and kissed me—tickled my belly and made me laugh? How often had she told me stories late at night, after the men had gone, to help me sleep? I could see her face clearly now in my mind's eye, the way it had come to me in nightmares, but for the first time I realised how young she looked. She must have been a teenager when she had me. No more than her early twenties when she left me.

The soreness in my throat began to choke me.

'Dio!' I swore softly against Edie's hair as I clung to her. 'How could I not have seen this before?' I said, but I knew why. Because I had been determined not to see it, not to trust, not to love, so I could protect myself at all costs. It's why I had always rejected the truth about my mother, and why I had treated Edie so appallingly. 'I have been blaming my selfishness and my cowardice on her when the person who is truly responsible is me.'

Edie grasped my cheeks and forced my gaze to meet hers, until she was staring me straight in the eyes. The love I saw there humbled me.

'That's rubbish, Dante,' she said. And I almost laughed at the fierceness in her tone. 'You're a good man.'

No, I wasn't. But if she believed it, it was enough. At this point, I really didn't care if I deserved her or not. I would take anything I could get. Anything that she would give me and thank God for it always.

'You were scared and, after what happened with your mum,' she added, still fierce, still determined to see the best in me, 'it makes sense you would push me away.'

'Are you saying you forgive me, *bella*?' I asked, ready to believe in miracles.

The torment of the last few minutes, the last few hours and days and weeks melted away as her lips curved into the sweet smile I had become addicted to.

Warmth spread through me. She was going to give me a second chance. I could see it in her eyes. *Dio*, but she was utterly adorable. What on earth had I done to deserve her? And what wouldn't I do to keep her?

'What do you think?' she said as she wrapped her arms around my neck and lifted her lips to mine.

I didn't need another invitation.

I grasped her hips and captured her mouth, thrusting my tongue deep, determined to claim her, to brand her as mine for all eternity.

CHAPTER TWENTY-THREE

DANTE'S MOUTH CRUSHED mine as hope and excitement and a deep welling tenderness blossomed inside my heart.

He'd come to me, he'd told me he loved me, he'd even told me about his mother—a subject I knew it was very difficult for him to discuss. We were equals. We had a chance now to make this something good and strong, solid and lasting. And I intended to grab that chance with both hands.

I sank into the kiss, need arrowing through me as the prominent outline of his erection pressed against my belly. Even through our clothing, the thick ridge felt powerful and potent. My sex softened, ready to receive it.

'You will come back to work at The Inferno? And live with me at La Villa Paradis?' he murmured as his lips caressed my neck and his hands cupped my bottom.

'Yes, yes…' Joy surged through me at his offer. I wanted to be with him more than anything in the world. And I loved the work I had been doing at the casino. 'But…' I tore myself away from him to look into his eyes '…you must promise never to freak out like that again when I'm working.'

'Of course, I would never freak out at *you*, *bella*,' he said instantly. A flush of heat—and stunned pleasure—spread up my torso and into my cheeks at his easy capitulation and the evidence that he respected me, professionally as well as personally. But then he added, 'But Galanti is a dead man if he ever smiles at you like that again.'

'Dante, that's mad,' I said, because I could see he wasn't entirely joking. 'You can't kill Mr Galanti for smiling at me. It would be very bad for business.'

But, before I could argue further, he captured the pulse point in my collarbone with his lips and suckled strongly. Arousal shot through me as the liquid tug in my abdomen became a definite yank. And my mind blurred on my last coherent thought.

Welcome to The Inferno, indeed!

EPILOGUE

'THAT WAS JOE. We've finalised the training course,' I clicked off my smartphone and shouted to Dante above the hum of the helicopter blades as the big black bird came in to land on La Villa Paradis's heliport. 'By the end of this year we should have all the casino staff trained on how to stop the different systems I've uncovered,' I added proudly, pleased with everything I'd achieved in my role as Allegri's Head of Gaming Systems and Security.

'Excellent work, *bella*,' Dante said as he unclipped his seat belt and mine while the helicopter's blades swished to a stop. But then he scooped my phone out of my hands and tucked it in his back pocket. 'But there is to be no more shop talk now for the rest of the weekend,' he said as he hauled me out of my seat and into his arms. 'Or I will have to fire you.'

'Go ahead,' I teased back as I banded my arms around his lean waist. 'I know several other casino owners who would hire me in a second.'

'Then they would have to die,' he said before leaning down to cover my lips in a possessive kiss.

The kiss went from amused to carnal in seconds—as it always did with Dante—but just as I became desperate, the heat burning up my torso like wildfire, he pulled away from me, ducked down and hefted me onto his shoulder in a fireman's lift.

'What are you doing?' I demanded, suddenly staring at the tight muscles of his backside outlined in worn denim—as he hauled me off the helicopter like a sack of potatoes. 'Put me down,' I added, but my protests lacked heat, thanks to the laughter bubbling out of my mouth.

'Be still, woman,' he said, giving me a playful pat on my bottom. 'Or I'll drop you.'

Ignoring my struggles, Dante marched past the pilot and Collette and her staff, who were watching our antics with amusement. But, instead of heading into the house and straight up to our suite, as I had expected, he walked in the opposite direction, around the side of the chateau, then through the grounds, past the fountains and the follies and the Japanese pagoda. I had to stop struggling, scared he might drop me for real, as he carried me down the steps to our private beach.

The sun heated my skin and my heart swelled in my chest as I finally landed on my feet again—in our special place.

It was over a year since we'd first made love in this cove and we always found time to christen it again whenever we escaped to La Villa Paradis from our work in Monaco. It had been a year filled with love and light and laughter, and the occasional passionate argument, because Dante was still the most infuriating man I'd ever met. As well as the most wonderful.

'You're a menace,' I said, with no heat whatsoever. 'I can't believe you just carried me off like that in front of the staff. As if you were a pirate and I was your captive! They'll never take me seriously again.'

'The staff adore you, as you well know,' he chastised me, the twinkle of mischief in his eyes suggesting my punishment wasn't over yet. A giddy thrill careered through my system. 'And if you don't want to be treated like a captive then don't threaten to leave me.'

My cheeks flushed as he captured my face in his palms, his fingers caressing my neck and sending erotic shivers to the rest of my body.

'You know it makes me crazy,' he murmured and I realised the playful spark had disappeared.

'You know I'd never leave you,' I said. Surely he knew I had only been joking?

A sensual smile spread across his lips and relief flooded through my system.

'I know,' he said. 'But I think it is time we made that official. And I wanted to bring you here to make that happen.'

Huh?

My eyes widened as he reached into the front pocket of his jeans and produced a small velvet box. He flipped it open to reveal a ring nestled in black velvet—a white gold band studded with tiny emeralds which sparkled in the sunlight.

My sight blurred and my heart bounced up to bump my tonsils as he sunk to one knee on the sand in front of me.

'My love, my life, my *bella*,' he said, his voice gruff and deadly serious now. 'Will you become my wife?'

I covered my mouth with quivering fingers as tears of joy seeped over my lids to course down my cheeks—so shocked and moved I could barely speak. 'Oh, Dante, I… I… I can't…'

'All you have to do is say yes, *bella*,' he said gently, the tiny quiver of uncertainty as his gaze met mine making me love him all the more.

'Oh, Dante…' I said again. And then I flew at him, throwing my arms around his shoulders and knocking him over. 'Yes, yes, yes!' I shouted, so the whole world could hear me. And him most of all. 'Absolutely yes!'

His deep chuckles joined my joyous laughter as we rolled over together.

The sun shone on his waves of dark hair as he rose over me. 'Damn, I think I've lost the ring,' he said as he glanced at the now empty ring box still clutched in his fist.

'It doesn't matter,' I said, flinging my arms around his neck to pull him down towards me. 'We'll find it, together.'

He smiled at me, the cool blue of his irises hot with the promise of all the years to come. 'Yes,' he said, his voice rich and full of confidence—like my heart. 'We will find it, together.'

Then he kissed me, and his lips tasted of safety and security, and love, and sunshine, and happiness… And sand!

* * * * *

MILLS & BOON

Coming next month

A CINDERELLA TO SECURE HIS HEIR
Michelle Smart

'Do not misunderstand me. Getting custody of Domenico is my primary motivation. He is a Palvetti and he deserves to take his place with us, his family. In my care he can have everything but if custody were all I wanted, he would already be with me.'

She took another sip of her drink. Normally she hated whisky in any of its forms but right then the burn it made in her throat was welcome. It was the fire she needed to cut through her despair. 'Then what *do* you want? I think of all the work we've done, all the hours spent, all the money spent–'

'I wanted to get to know you.'

She finally allowed herself to look at him. '*Why*?'

The emerald eyes that had turned her veins to treacle lasered into hers. He leaned forward and spoke quietly. 'I wanted to learn about you through more than the reports and photographs my investigators provided me with.'

'You had me investigated?'

'I thought it prudent to look into the character of the person caring for my nephew.'

Her head span so violently she felt dizzy with the motion.

He'd been spying on her.

She should have known Alessio's silence since she'd refused his offer of money in exchange for Dom had been ominous. She'd lulled herself into a false sense of security and underestimated him and underestimated the lengths he would be prepared to go to.

Everything Domenico had said about his brother was true, and more.

Through the ringing in her ears, he continued. 'Do not worry. Any childhood indiscretions are your own concern. I only wanted to know about the last five years of your life and what I learned about you intrigued me. It was clear to me from the investigators' reports and your refusal of my financial offer that you had an affection for my nephew...'

'Affection does not cover a fraction of the love I feel for him,' she told him fiercely.

'I am beginning to understand that for myself.'

'Good, because I will never let him go without a fight.'

'I understand that too but you must know that if it came to a fight, you would never win. I could have gone through the British courts and made my case for custody—I think we are both aware that my wealth and power would have outmatched your efforts—but Domenico is familiar with you and it is better for him if you remain in his life than be cut off.'

She held his gaze and lifted her chin. 'I'm all he knows.'

He raised a nonchalant shoulder. 'But he is very young. If it comes to it, he will adapt without you quickly. For the avoidance of doubt, I do not want that outcome.'

'What outcome *do* you want?'

'Marriage.'

Drum beats joined the chorus of sound in her head. 'What on *earth* are you talking about?'

He rose from his seat and headed back to the bar. 'Once I have Domenico in Milan it will be a simple matter for me to take legal guardianship of him.' He poured himself another large measure and swirled it in his glass. 'I recognise your genuine affection for each other and have no wish to separate you. In all our best interests, I am prepared to marry you.'

Dumbfounded, Beth shook her head, desperately trying to rid herself of all the noise in her ears so she could think properly. 'I wouldn't marry you if you paid me.'

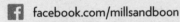